How to Catch a Thief

How to Catch a Thief

Austin Moon

How to Catch a Thief. Copyright © 2025 by Austin Moon.

Triomphe Press 2025

Cover illustration and design by Austin Moon

ISBN 978-1-958123-11-9

First Edition: March 2025

Printed in the United States of America

10 9 8 7 6 5 4 3 2

Mum, thanks for letting me watch scary detective shows when I was a kid even though they gave me nightmares. Look at me now!

PROLOGUE

"Please, have another drink." Dean tipped the champagne bottle until it poured into the man's glass.

"Oh, twist my arm," the southern gentleman replied in a thick drawl that informed everyone in the room he was not from Los Angeles. The man took a pull from the glass and puffed on his already lit cigar—even though Dean had previously told him that there was to be *no* smoking in the house. Though, he was sure the old Victorian lounge had seen its fair share of cigars and cigarettes throughout the years.

They were standing on one side of the space by the bar next to a couple of gold swivel stools—a modern element in an otherwise historically untouched room.

Dean grinned and waved the cloud of smoke away from his face with one hand. "You seem like a sensible gentleman, Mr. Hackney. What do you think of my proposal?"

Dean's friend Fern leaned closely against his shoulder. She was wearing a slinky metallic gold dress that hugged her cool brown skin, her honey blonde curls loose around her shoulders.

The businessman shrugged nonchalantly. "Well, you know I'll need to have the boys look it over for me. I don't do anything without the nerds giving it the okay."

"Really?" Dean narrowed his eyes and gave him a crooked smile. "I wouldn't expect that you allow anyone to tell you what to do with your business."

Mr. Hackney cleared his throat after taking another puff off his cigar. "I don't. The nerds are just my insurance policy. You can't be too careful in business, son."

Dean could tell that he was starting to chip away at the man's well-polished veneer. Even in the dimly lit lounge he noticed Mr. Hackney was flushed from the alcohol, his cheeks ruddy like a mall Santa.

"*Hmm.*" Dean turned his attention toward Fern in hopes of annoying Mr. Hackney further. "Felicity, how much did you say Mr.

Crandler made with us last year," he whispered, barely loud enough to be overheard. "Was it one point four?"

Fern smiled, enjoying their game of cat and mouse. "Did I say one point four? I thought I told you one point six. Maybe you misheard."

Dean curled his lips into a smirk. "Right. You did say that, didn't you? What would I do without you?"

She grinned with purple-tinted lips. "I shudder to think."

"Good thing I won't ever have to imagine, then." He clinked his champagne glass against hers and turned back to Mr. Hackney as if just remembering he was still in the room.

The businessman was puffing quickly on his cigar, the plumes of smoke swirling around his head. He plucked it from his mouth and downed what was left of his glass. "One point six, you say?"

Dean widened his eyes in faux surprise. "Oh, did you hear that? Sorry, I know you're not interested. I shouldn't have brought it up."

Mr. Hackney balked, opening and closing his mouth before finally saying, "How much risk is involved in this deal? You haven't exactly told me what it is."

Dean waved his hand through the air like it was a silly question. "I'd be taking on all the risk as the main investor, of course. I never leave my backers hanging. It's a simple import/export deal. We're investing in our own shipping lane of sorts to get around the main channels."

He narrowed his eyes. "So it's illegal?"

Dean shook his head and clucked his tongue. "Of course not, Mr. Hackney. What kind of businessman do you think I am? It's merely a work-around, a loophole. All perfectly legal."

Mr. Hackney's face was growing pinker by the minute, his brow glistening with sweat despite the air-conditioned lounge. The other guests of the party were milling around and talking in groups while catering staff brought out trays of finger foods and more alcohol.

He tugged at his collar. "And you say you already have other backers?"

Dean beamed. "Yes, we're looking for our lucky finalist. We already have six out of seven, including myself. I've always thought seven was a pretty lucky number, don't you, Mr. Hackney? It's never steered me wrong before."

The man licked his lips and wrung his hands together. "Who are these backers? Mr. Crandler?"

Dean sucked on his teeth. "You heard that too? I suppose the champagne is getting to me. I'm not usually so loose-lipped." He turned to Fern. "Who else do we have, darling? Mr. Sevigny, Councilman Crowder, Lady Vanquist."

She tapped his shoulder with a well-manicured hand. "Don't forget the Baroness of Strandholm."

"Ah yes, the Baroness. How could she have slipped my mind? Charming lady."

Mr. Hackney considered the other guests around the room. A woman with a full face of makeup was talking to a tall blond guy wearing a tailored maroon suit. A bear of a man with tattoos on his arms and exposed neck was drinking scotch near the edge of the room watching on with interest. "And what about these others? Have they all been offered the same deal?"

"Not specifically, no. You were our first pick, Mr. Hackney. We heard how much you value your investments. But, if you're not interested Mrs. Wong is next on our list, I'm sure she'd be more than happy to—"

"*No!,*" he barked. "I'll take you up on your offer, Mr. Prescott. How much time do I have to get everything together?"

Dean shrugged casually. "The end of the party, Mr. Hackney. This deal is moving quickly."

Mr. Hackney nodded. "Okay, you drive a hard bargain, but okay. I'll make some calls and get the funds together."

The corner of Dean's lip pulled up into a lopsided grin. "That's what I like to hear, Mr. Hackney. Felicity will give you all the necessary details. Let me refill your glass. It seems our bottle has run dry." He nodded to Fern and took Mr. Hackney's glass to the back of the room where the catering staff had set out the extra champagne on ice.

* * *

"Well, well, you've done it again, Dean." Fern was sitting on the piano bench in the lounge with a cheeky smile on her face.

Dean waved his hand through the air like *it's nothing*. "It was a team effort, Fern, you know that. You think I would have had Mr. Hackney eating out of my hand without your particular skill set?"

She frowned. "Do you mean my boobs?"

He laughed. "Of course not, I meant your charm and wit. Though your glamorous allure doesn't hurt either." He sat down beside her and threw an arm around her shoulders. "We're going big on this one, Fee. We might need to skip town for a couple months. Greece, maybe?"

She grinned. "I could go for Greece. It's so delicious in the summertime. We'd blend in beautifully with all the tourists, and of course, you know, lots of potential there."

Dean scoffed. "Nah, we're in the big leagues now, no more pickpocketing and grifting. It's not even worth our time."

She shrugged. "I suppose you're right. It's still fun, though. Like old times."

Dean took a sip of scotch from his tumbler and smiled, remembering.

"Are the caterers gone?" Fern asked.

"Yep, it's just us now. The cleaners aren't coming until the morning."

Fern stretched out and ran a hand through her golden curls. "You really do find the most amazing houses, Dean. I don't know how you do it."

He grinned. "Luck and determination."

"How long are we staying?"

He sucked on his teeth. "Well, the owner gets back in two weeks, but it's better to ditch it as soon as Mr. Hackney's wire transfer goes through. We don't want to spook him. We also don't want to be caught hanging around either."

"Got it." She nodded toward the door. "Are we going to head out?"

Dean sighed dramatically. "Oh, I suppose. If we *must*." He pulled himself off the piano bench and helped Fern to stand. He'd always thought high heels were a rather ridiculous invention even if she did look incredible in them. "I'm going to go around and check things one more time, make sure everything is secure, and then we can slip out quietly."

Fern took a few steps back into the open area of the room and performed a lazy twirl. "Okay, I'll be here."

Dean left the lounge with his glass of scotch and downed the last of it before wandering around the house. He was *technically* responsible for the security of the mansion, after all.

He whispered to himself as he checked every room, "Hallway clear. Bathroom empty. No one hanging around waiting to stab me in *this* dark corner."

He checked the kitchen, the butler's quarters, the empty, pristine dining room, and both of the downstairs sitting rooms. The last area to check in the west wing was the downstairs study. Though it was more of a library or museum than a true study. Dean slid the wooden pocket doors aside and took a peak around the space. All dark and quiet. "Okay."

He was sliding the doors closed when something caught his eye that made him pause. A small red flickering light at the back of the room. He'd almost missed it if it wasn't for the darkness. "What do we have here?" He pushed the doors open once more and grazed the wall with his hand, looking for the light switch. There.

The overhead chandelier illuminated the spacious, yet full, study. He searched for the red light again and paled when he caught sight of it. "*Shit, shit, shit.*" He ran across the Turkish carpet and stopped in front of the grand fireplace at the back of the room. There was an empty space in the center of the mantel where there had previously been an ornate, gold statue of a cat. Dean had noted the antiquity in his initial security assessment days ago. The red light was still blinking. *Why had the alarm not gone off?*

"FERN!"

"Yeah?" she called from the other room.

He pulled his fingers through his dark locks. "We got a problem!"

She walked in through the open doorway, her arms crossed over her middle. "What kind of problem?"

He gestured to the mantel, his chest filling with dread. "A big one."

ONE

Something wet and sticky was touching my cheek. I blinked open one eye and caught sight of a furry, black mass. My throat was dry and aching, and my eyes burned from the early morning light streaking in through my bedroom windows.

"Good morning, Captain," I mumbled into the pillow before wiping the wet dog drool from my face. Captain panted with his tongue hanging from his mouth and pushed his muzzle into my neck.

"Five more minutes," I pleaded, knowing it was futile. Captain was strong willed and didn't take no for an answer. He licked my face some more, this time reaching my ear, making me squirm.

"Okay, okay, I'm getting up." I pushed myself into a sitting position and dared to open both eyes. "Coffee first, okay bud? Then we can go on a W-A-L-K." I knew saying the word itself would send him into a frenzy, so I avoided it at all costs.

I pulled on a mostly clean, dark t-shirt I found on the floor and wandered into the small bathroom to do what ninety-nine percent of people do first thing in the morning. Then I splashed some ice-cold water on my face to wake me up. The bright sting was invigorating, and the only thing besides Captain keeping me from falling back into bed.

When I finished in the bathroom I wandered toward the nightstand and slipped on the watch my parents had given me for graduating high school. It was hard to ignore the gold ring that sat in a ceramic bowl next to the small side lamp. I still couldn't bring myself to get rid of it, and my muscle memory reached to slip it on after I put on my watch. *Every. Single. Day.*

"Coffee," I reminded myself, moving out of the small bedroom that barely fit my mattress and into the even smaller kitchen with its two-burner hot plate and microwave. I opened the upper cabinet and pulled down the round tin of coffee from the shelf. It was suspiciously light. *"Oh, come on."* I opened the lid and sure enough. Empty. I sighed, glancing over at the grocery list hanging on the fridge that I'd never picked up. "Dammit." I turned to look down at the expectant Captain. "I guess you get your wish, buddy. Let's go. Grab your lead."

Captain raced down the short hallway to the door where I kept his leash on the wall. He brought it back dutifully, wagging his fluffy black tail without a care in the world.

"Well you don't have to be so smug about it," I mumbled as I attached the lead to his collar. "Give me two seconds, okay?" I threw on some black joggers from my closet that I was sixty percent sure were clean, along with an old pair of black sneakers. I made sure to grab my wallet, keys, and phone. I *never* left the house unprepared. "Okay, let's go."

Captain was already waiting beside the door, the other side of the leash in his mouth. "Thanks, Captain. *Good boy.*" I grabbed the strap and opened the door to the skinny stairwell. Captain leaped down the steps faster than I could keep up, down to the bottom floor and out the back door leading to the street.

Los Angeles was already buzzing with activity early in the morning, though the city never *truly* slept. Club kids were coming home from West Hollywood and early morning surfers were heading out to Venice Beach and Malibu.

Captain was eager to run, however I was *not* in the mood. I hobbled and hopped as he jerked on his leash. We went around the block twice—Captain marked his territory in the usual spot—and then we headed inside Greta's Diner on the corner. Why it was called that I could never figure out. The owner was named Rosalie and she had inherited the place from a Herbert who had bought it from an old Greek family. No Gretas.

Greta's Diner was, *how to put it*, kinda shit. However, they allowed me to bring Captain inside, work as late as I wanted, and always refilled my cup with more coffee—even if it *was* less than stellar coffee.

I sat down in my usual booth in the back and settled in with Captain resting down below at my feet.

Hey, Mr. Detective," Rosalie greeted without looking up from her phone. She must have noticed Captain running along in front of me. He was pretty hard to miss. "What'll it be?"

"Just coffee, thanks."

She waved her hand and left to grab the coffee pot from the front counter, all without looking up from her screen. I was impressed at how efficient she had become at doing as little as possible. Rosalie was a waif of a woman with curly gray hair always up in a messy bun and a smoker's voice. She'd owned Greta's diner since the nineties when the area was pretty dangerous and she'd survived through it all.

With nothing to do while I waited I quickly checked my email on my phone and then the private message box on my website. Nothing. Work had been slow lately, or always. It was hard to tell the difference. In the age of internet research and quick answers not many people could justify the decision to hire a private detective. Everyone thought they were some kind of an amateur sleuth, nowadays.

I sighed and ran a hand across my short crop of dark, spiky hair. The barber had cut it too short last week and I looked like a punk. I didn't mind exactly, if it meant people left me alone. It wasn't necessarily a bad thing in my line of work to look intimidating. I just wasn't used to it.

"Here you go." Rosalie poured some strong black coffee into my empty cup and turned away without saying another word. Even though she wasn't warm and fuzzy, I could tell she cared about her regular customers, she treated them like siblings that she both resented yet loved. That's why I liked Greta's Diner. It reminded me of my grandparents' Korean restaurant and all the good memories I had hanging out there as a child. It felt more like a place you actually wanted to spend time at instead of some soulless dime-a-dozen franchise.

The place was pretty empty for a Saturday morning with only a couple other diners—an old man reading the newspaper with a stack of donuts and a young woman and her child eating a massive stack of pancakes covered in whipped cream. At least *someone* was having a good day.

I needed clients and I needed them *now*. My last case had wrapped up three days ago—a simple cheating job. I took them when I needed to even though they weren't my favorite. Because no matter the result clients are always unhappy, and somehow that unhappiness always managed to land on me.

In this particular case, the woman's husband was driving two hours every Friday afternoon to hook up with an old flame from college. Sad business, but I only give them the results. It isn't my fault that they ask the question. Though, if I was being cheated on of course I would want to know. There's really no safety in hiding from the truth. Only prolonged heartbreak.

I took a long pull of coffee and let it simmer its way into my brain, waking up my senses. Thank God for the little things.

My phone buzzed. I lifted it eagerly, hoping for once it was a client and not a bill or spam. *Worse.* It was my mother.

M: Noah, are you free on Tuesday? Your brother and the family are going to come over for dinner.

While that may have seemed like a pretty normal request, what she was *really* asking me to do was sit around while her and my father asked me a million questions about my job and dragged out all their usual arguments as to why I should sell the business and get a real job as a lawyer—like my parents had always wanted.

No. Time to come up with an excuse. Unfortunately, I didn't have any active clients right now. Did I bluff? Or come up with a completely different excuse? I also couldn't simply ignore it. She'd send the feds to my door, claiming I'd been killed or kidnapped. She was a fearsome woman who didn't take no for an answer.

N: Super busy right now, Mom. Working on a big case. I don't think I'll be able to make it.

I hesitated over the send button before launching it into the ether. More than likely this would result in a text from my brother and maybe even one from my father if I was unlucky.

I took another long drink of the black coffee, finishing off the cup. It would have to do. Better to be in the office, even if I was only keeping up the illusion of hard work. My ex would say that staying busy prompted the universe that you were ready for more. If you believed in stuff like that. I never quite got down with Malcolm's bullshit, but the main principle still made sense to me. Better to stay busy than idle.

I paid for my coffee by placing a bill on the counter in front of Rosalie. "Thanks, come again," she mumbled, all the while staring down at her phone.

"Come on, Captain." I ushered the black labradoodle outside onto the sidewalk and guided him down the street back to the apartment. The apartment that stood over my business, The Golden Sun Detective Agency.

I passed the gold placard on the outside wall and into the small lobby, beginning the walk up the short flight of stairs to unlock the office doors. We got some of our best clients on weekends, surprisingly. I was counting on that. *Wishing* for it, really.

Captain raced up the steps in front of me and nudged open the door to the office. I hadn't unlocked it yet. *Did I forget last night?* I didn't normally forget important things like that.

Had someone broken in? How could they, the outside door was still secure? I slowly climbed up the last couple steps to the open doorway and peered inside. Captain wasn't barking. Not that he was much of a guard dog, he was too friendly and lovable to attack or defend.

"*There* you are. Slacking again, Uncle Noah?" a chipper, yet sarcastic voice called out to me.

I let out a sigh of relief. Not a break-in, then. Only my niece, Lexi, who worked for me sometimes on the weekends.

"Slacking?" I checked my watch one more time, it was barely scraping eight o'clock. "Why are you here so early, huh? Avoiding your dad?" My brother Mark was a bit domineering when it came to running his household. The only reason he allowed Lexi to do some *light secretarial* work for me was because he was under the impression that she was mostly studying, doing her homework, and focusing on her college applications. Not booking clients and doing research for me. It was our little secret. However, there was no reason for anyone to worry, I paid her for her talents. She made sure of it.

"How'd you guess?" she said with an eye roll, rubbing Captain behind his ears.

I walked in and crouched beside the front desk to scratch Captain in a team effort. "I don't know how much there's going to be to do around here today. We don't have any clients scheduled." Not that I didn't enjoy her company regardless.

Lexi frowned. "Then what do you call the rich guy waiting in your office?"

"*Hmm?*" I turned to look in that direction, but the blinds were covering the window. "We have a walk-in?" I tried to mask my surprise and, no doubt, failed miserably.

Lexi nodded. "Dressed super nice too—Rolex, Prada, you name it."

"How long has he been waiting?"

"I was about to text you, so only a couple minutes. He was waiting outside when I got here, and even though I told him you were out, he insisted that he'd wait as long as he needed."

"*Huh.* So what's the story? Did he say anything?"

She shook her head, pulling a long strand of dark hair behind her ear. "No. He was cagey to talk to me about it. Not nervous exactly, just that he wanted to keep it private."

"*Hmm*, okay. Thanks." I glanced down at myself, remembering that I was wearing sweats. "Can you keep Captain entertained for me?"

She smiled and rubbed Captain's fluffy face. "Of course."

I jogged to the closet at the back of the room where I kept an extra coat —black leather. It wouldn't hide the sweatpants, but it would hopefully

17

make me look a little less ruffled and sleepy. I pulled a hand through my buzzed hair, again forgetting that there was nothing to do about it. Hopefully I looked okay, not that I was obsessed with appearance, however rich people didn't like hiring slobs.

"How do I look?" I asked Lexi quietly.

She appraised me and then gave me the thumbs up. "As good as it's going to get."

I laughed through my nose. "Thanks, kid."

She beamed. "You're welcome. Now get in there. Don't want to keep the man waiting."

A client in a suit. A client with a *Rolex*. This was good. We needed this. I took in a deep breath and steadied myself before making my way over to my office. I hoped he wasn't offended that he'd had to wait. We were called Golden Sun for a reason—not only was Sun my last name, but it was also an assurance that we'd work day and night to solve your case, sunup to sundown.

I opened the door and slipped inside. "Hello, sorry to keep you waiting, it's been a hectic morning."

The man rose from his seat and turned to face me. He was young—though it was hard to clock his age, maybe late twenties or early thirties—with a short crop of lacquered brown hair combed with expert precision and dark brown eyes. His suit was a crisp navy coordinated with a cherry-red tie.

"It was no problem at all. I told the girl out front that I'd wait all day if I had to." He smiled, though I could tell it was one of geniality rather than joy. Not only was he well dressed, he was also quite handsome with a strong jaw, rounded chin, and straight nose. *Definitely* old money. Probably East Coast, though I couldn't tell where his accent was coming from yet.

I held out my hand. "I'm Detective Sun, and you are?"

He returned the gesture, his grip firm and warm. "Dean Prescott, Mr. Sun. Nice to meet you, though the circumstances could be better."

"Yes, hardly anyone comes to me with good news, unfortunately. What seems to be the problem, Mr. Prescott?"

He grimaced. "I've been robbed."

TWO

"Please, have a seat." I directed him to the plush chair in front of my desk where he'd already been waiting.

I sat down across from him in my old leather desk chair and pulled out my notebook to jot down his information.

He sat and crossed his legs, lacing his hands together on top of his knee. "I'll get right to the point, then, since I don't want to waste any time. Someone stole something very valuable from me last night and I need to get it back as quickly as possible."

"I see." Thank God this wasn't another cheating case, however I would find it hard to believe that someone would cheat on Mr. Rolex, solely based on his wealth and his jawline. Though, I was aware that looks could be deceiving.

"Or I should say, my *uncle's* house has been robbed. I've been house sitting for him while he's traveling around the Mediterranean, and last night I threw a party. Sometime during the event someone stole a horribly expensive statue from my uncle's office."

"Okay." I stopped writing. "And why come to me? Why not the police?"

He tugged at his collar with a finger. "To be honest with you, Mr. Sun, my uncle is getting up there in years and if I involve the police I would have to tell him about the missing statue, and I'm afraid he would have a stroke or a heart attack, something terrible. No, I would much prefer hiring someone to find the statue before he gets back so that he will never have to know it was gone in the first place."

I'm *sure* that's all it was, concern for his uncle's health, and *not* getting in major trouble for being careless. Typical trust fund kid behavior.

"I understand. Okay, so tell me a little bit more about this party. Was it a large gathering?"

He shook his head. "No, quite the opposite, actually, there were only about ten of us in attendance, plus the staff."

"And what specifically was stolen? What's the value?"

Dean laughed awkwardly and leaned forward. "Well, it's a priceless Egyptian antiquity that my uncle acquired from his grandfather who had brought it back from Egypt in the 1920s. It's a golden cat statue inlaid with rubies—part of a pair. The legend is that the statue's twin has been lost for centuries." He shook his head in apparent disbelief. "I want to say that the thing is worth at least four million, though I don't think my uncle ever truly had it appraised. He didn't care about the monetary value of his collection. Maybe his insurance people know."

"Four million dollars?" That was a hefty payday for a would-be thief.

He nodded, his camera-ready smile dropping slightly. "Yes, so you can see I'm in a bit of a pickle here."

I put down my notebook, slipped my laptop out of its case, and placed it on the desk.

He laughed through his nose. "I see I've been upgraded."

I tried to stay professional even as I cracked a smile. "Well, yes. Quite frankly that's quite a large sum of money, Mr. Prescott."

"Are you used to these types of cases? Theft, I mean."

I nodded assuringly. "Extremely. It's the bread and butter of the trade, that and marital issues." After my laptop booted up I opened a new case file and shared the document with Lexi. "Can I ask how you found our agency, Mr. Prescott? There are many other agencies in Los Angeles."

His smile dipped, his brows pulling together. "Yes, well, I believe that you can be very discreet? If I'm being honest with you, Mr. Sun, I was worried that if I went to a larger firm there would be more eyes and ears on my case. I don't need the media catching wind of this, it would break my uncle's heart as I've already explained."

Ah, now I understood. He hadn't chosen us because he thought we were more qualified, he'd chosen us because he saw us as small potatoes. Easier to control. He wanted the assurance that we wouldn't sell his information to the press. "I see. That's all I needed to know. Let's get down to it, shall we?"

He nodded and crossed his legs again. "Yes."

I typed out a short description of the stolen statue and a few key details about Mr. Prescott that he'd already shared with me. "So, how confident are you that the statue was stolen during this party? Could it have been missing before? Or after?"

He shook his head. "Absolutely not. My uncle's house has *very* tight security. Or...it usually does." He cringed. "I gave the security guard the week off so that I could entertain some new business acquaintances while I was watching the place."

"And did you know any of these guests prior to the party or were they all strangers to you?"

He thought a moment before he said, "I suppose they were all strangers, everyone except for my friend Felicity. She was there with me as well."

"So how can you be certain that the statue was taken during the party if you sent your security home early?" I asked. It seemed like a pretty idiotic thing to do when you were inviting guests over to what I was sure was a multi-million dollar mansion. What had he *really* been up to? He was holding something back.

"Because I gave security the night off I walked the entirety of the house myself, before *and* after the event. That's how I realized the statue was gone in the first place. Usually if the statue were to be moved even a millimeter an alarm would go off and the police would instantly be called, however the alarm must have been tampered with."

"So the statue was there right before your party began?" I confirmed.

He nodded. "Yes."

"Okay, this is good. We have a short timeline and a small pool of suspects, it seems. Those are both odds in your favor, though I have to be frank with you. Your statue could be selling on the underground market at this very minute. Once it changes hands it's almost impossible to get back, even if you involve the police."

Dean clasped his hands and fiddled with a ring on his left pointer finger. "I'm aware of that, Mr. Sun. That's why I came as soon as possible."

I supposed that explained the early morning walk-in, then. "Okay, as long as you understand."

I had typed out a few more lines on the document in front of me when Lexi's pink text popped up below my own asking if I wanted her to help. Would he care? Did it matter if my kid niece knew about his troubles?

"Do you mind if my research assistant takes notes during our meeting? It would be faster that way and your case appears to be pretty time-sensitive."

He pointed behind him with his thumb. "The girl?"

I nodded.

He squirmed. "Is she...also discreet?"

I grinned confidently. "Don't worry, Mr. Prescott, Lexi doesn't spend her free time gossiping on social media. She's a Yale hopeful." That was a stretch. Her parents *hoped* that she was a Yale hopeful, however it still seemed to put him at ease.

I typed out a reply in the document and she knocked on the door half a second later. She entered with a no-nonsense expression. "I've finished filing Captain Yoon's paperwork, Mr. Sun."

"Ah, good." Quick-thinking Lexi had taken Captain back up to the apartment, most likely to eat some breakfast. I hoped he wouldn't destroy the place while I was gone. The last time I'd left him alone too long while working a case he'd chewed up all my toilet paper.

She took the seat beside mine at the edge of the desk and opened her own laptop to start typing. I gave her a quick overview about what we'd been discussing for Mr. Prescott's benefit, although she'd already read my notes.

"Wow, that's bad." Lexi wasn't known for her subtlety.

I smiled to lighten the mood. "Let's get back to it. Mr. Prescott, can you tell us who all you invited to your uncle's house last night?"

He cringed. "Well, yes and no."

I raised an eyebrow. "*Yes and no?*"

"As I said, the event was to meet some new investors and I'm not sure how many of them want you to know that they were there. My investors expect total privacy."

Lexi turned to me and rolled her eyes away from his gaze.

I smiled. "I'm not sure how you want me to go about investigating this stolen statue if I can't look into the people you suspect of stealing it?"

He shifted in his seat, crossed his legs the opposite way, and cleared his throat. "Well, I was hoping you could maybe take a look around the house and figure out *how* the person did it and *that* would lead you to the thief."

"That's not how I work." I shook my head. "That would be very much putting the cart before the horse, if you catch my drift. The *who* is a little more important than the *how*, wouldn't you say?"

He pinched his brows together. "I...suppose I understand what you're saying. Forgive me, I don't know how this whole investigation thing works. I've never hired a detective before."

"It's understandable." I smiled. "You'd be surprised how many clients I get that expect me to act like their favorite TV show characters. Unfortunately life doesn't work out like it does on TV."

I took a look at Lexi's laptop screen. She'd already rewritten and formatted my sloppy notes into a readable standardized layout. I had to hand it to the kid. I wouldn't know how to cope without her.

"I suppose as long as we're being discreet here...I can tell you *some* names. I guess the reason I brought up the house is because that's the part that boggles me the most. It's not the idea that a stranger would steal from me—I can imagine that easily—it's *how* they possibly had the time and ability to."

"We'll get to the bottom of it, don't worry, Mr. Prescott."

He let out a great big sigh and started to tally off on his fingers. "So there was me, obviously, and my friend Felicity as I've already mentioned. Then there was the catering staff, Rosewood Catering Company. I don't know any of their names, but there was a cook and two servers—a man and a woman." He caught my eye. "Do you think it was more likely that it was someone on the staff rather than a guest?"

I shrugged. "I never like to make assumptions, Mr. Prescott. Especially since you say that most, or all, of your guests were strangers to you. That adds a whole extra layer to this case."

He frowned. "Oh, I see what you mean. I think."

I waved my hand. "Please go on."

"There was Mr. Daryl Hackney and Mrs. Cassidy Wong, however I would find it hard to believe that it was either of them."

I raised an eyebrow. "And why is that?"

He shrugged. "Well...they're both quite rich, I think. What motive would they have to steal my uncle's statue?"

"*Hmm*, and yet you also said that you don't know either of them all that well."

"Yes I did, you're right."

"Who else was there?" I indicated to Lexi to keep typing. I could see she was already researching the first two names over on the side. She loved finding people online. She was always telling me how stupid the average person was about how much of their private information they put on social media.

"*Hmm*, that's where it starts to get hazy. Felicity would remember better than me. I know there was a young upstart there, I think his name was Miguel something or other, he worked in real estate. Then there was another young guy named Conrad. I can't remember if that was a first or last name." He gazed up at the ceiling and pursed his lips in concentration.

"You invited these people to your house and you don't even know their names?" Lexi asked before I could stop her.

"*Lexi,*" I said under my breath.

Luckily, Dean laughed, showing his wide smile of white teeth. "I guess so. I think that's why it might be best to check out the scene of the crime first and work backwards."

I hesitated. That was *not* how I usually operated, but if this trust fund kid couldn't get his shit together, it might be our best option. "I guess we could do that. Maybe you can call your friend and have her meet us back at the office when we're done at the house? We need those names."

He nodded. "Yes, I could do that. Let me go give her a quick call." He rose from his seat and smiled before slipping out the office door.

"Something stinks," Lexi said as soon as he was out of earshot.

I nodded slowly. "I know. He's definitely hiding something."

She raised an eyebrow. "Do you think he's playing dumb or is he the genuine article?"

"I can't tell quite yet. He's definitely rich; he has trust fund written all over him. He might be stressing now, but he has that relaxed personality of someone who's never had to work for anything in his life."

Lexi narrowed her eyes in the direction of the closed door. "*Hmm.*"

"What?"

"Are you sure you want to take this case?"

I almost laughed. "Are you worried about me?"

Lexi rolled her eyes and crossed her arms over her chest. "I'm worried about *the agency*. What if he screws you over?"

I grinned. "I'm a big kid, Lexi. I can take care of myself. I agree that something feels off here, but I can handle it. Besides, once we pry the rest of the details out of him it seems like a pretty simple case of theft. We might not be able to find the statue, however we can still earn a fat check for trying."

She shrugged. "It's your decision, boss."

I smirked. "I love when you call me boss."

"Well don't get used to it, Uncle Noah." She scoffed. "I was feeling generous. It won't happen again."

"Yeah, yeah." I swiveled my chair to look at her laptop screen better. "I saw you were already looking for some of the names. Find anything interesting?"

Lexi clicked through her browser tabs. "*Huh*, he was right about one thing: both Daryl Hackney and Cassidy Wong are multi-millionaires. The types you'd find on a Forbes list. Mr. Hackney owns a national hardware store chain with profits in the billions and Mrs. Wong is in the diamond trade. At first glance, neither seem like likely suspects. I'll know more in an hour."

"Okay, you keep on this while I go look at the house. See if you can find those other two names as well."

"Already on it." She switched tabs again. She'd found a social media page for a Miguel Gomez.

"Wow, over a million followers." I leaned in closer. "What does he do?"

She scrolled down the feed. "Sells real estate in the hills and shows off." In his most popular video he was revving a yellow sports car until smoke was billowing across the screen and then he sped off down the road.

"So an idiot, then."

"Basically." She typed something into her notes. "I'll work on finding the other guy while you're out."

"Okay. We shouldn't be gone too long. I doubt this will be terribly fruitful, but *if the client insists.*"

Lexi smiled as wide as she could and said in a high pitched retail voice, "*Then the client gets what they want.*"

I snapped my fingers. "*Exactly.*"

The door cracked open and I hid my joy, masking it with a professional, guarded expression. "Did you reach her?"

Dean smiled. "Yes, I'll pick her up after we're done."

"Okay, great. Now I just need you to put down a deposit for my services and then I can get started."

He nodded. "Oh, right. How does a private detective charge, anyway?" he asked, seeming genuinely curious.

I laid it out for him, leaning against the back of the desk. "I charge by the day and by the hour, including any incurred expenses. The deposit is calculated as twenty percent of how much time I think the case will take. In this case I'm expecting at least two days, but it could take longer than that. Are you paying check or card?"

He smiled. "Card is fine." He pulled a card out of his wallet and passed it on to Lexi to process.

"Great, and then if you can give me the address I'll meet you at the house."

He waved his hand. "Oh, I'll drive you."

I stopped myself from frowning. "You don't need to do that. I have a car." I might not have been rich, but my car was *mostly* reliable.

"I figured. This will be easier since the house is kinda hard to get to. It's easy to get lost up in the hills."

I forced a smile. "Okay, if you think that's best."

This guy was starting to get on my nerves. Did he think I would be blindly following his lead on this investigation? If so, he was in for a rude awakening. I didn't need a sidekick, and my patience only ran so deep.

I was already wearing my coat, so I only had to grab my notebook and my phone. I started to follow him out the door but stopped at the threshold, turning back to Lexi. "Call me if anything comes up."

She kept her eyes on her screen. "Will do."

I found Dean waiting for me downstairs, looking out of place with his suit and tie in the middle of the worn-down foyer.

"Shall we?" he asked, his hand perched on the door handle.

I smiled and gestured with my arm. "Yes, lead the way."

He opened the door and I trailed him across the pavement. The agency didn't have space for a parking lot, only street parking. My own car was parked around the back of the building by the dumpster to free up space, though most of the street was already filled up for the overhyped, pricy donut shop across the street.

"Which one is yours?" I asked absentmindedly, not paying attention until he pointed out the pale blue Porsche Speedster parked along the curb.

"Isn't she a beauty?" he asked with the smile of a proud child.

"Uh, yes, very nice." The top was already down and Dean hopped in without opening the door, then pushed open the passenger side for me.

I didn't know what I'd been expecting, but it wasn't that. The Speedster was obviously an expensive car, likely from the late fifties; I'd assumed most trust fund kids owned all the latest models like that guy Miguel.

"Seatbelt tight?" he asked with a grin as he turned over the engine.

"*Why?*" I asked warily.

The car lurched forward, pulling away from the curb at fifty miles an hour.

"That's why!" he yelled over the roar of the engine.

God, what had I gotten myself into?

THREE

The Hollywood strip blurred past us as we zipped through the west side of town and into the hills. Dean was a nauseating driver. He revved his engine, sped through intersections, took turns way too fast, and he kept looking back to smile or say something pithy about people he knew in the area instead of looking at the road. Why had I agreed to ride along with him?

We passed not one, not two, but three guard stations with locked gates before we reached his uncle's neighborhood high above the city. The area was everything I'd expected. Large castle-like houses in various shades of khaki sat on the sloped hillside with their long driveways and manicured lawns of green grass. Because screw the drought, right?

"What exactly does your uncle do for work, Mr. Prescott?" I asked for something to say. I wasn't terribly extroverted, however I definitely didn't enjoy being talked *at* instead of being part of the conversation, and Dean *really* loved talking. Plus, I was genuinely curious. I didn't *need* to know the answer for the case. I'd just always wondered how the rich in LA managed to stay so damn rich.

He looked back and grinned, his dark hair barely moving even with the wind. "So, my great-grandfather on my father's side is where it all starts. He made his legacy by building and operating a majority of the train lines from California to the South-West. My uncle made his mark in shipping and trading. His company controls a few shipping lanes between California and South America. It was an advantageous marriage between his sister—my mother—and the Prescotts. My father always joked that our family controlled both the land and the sea." He laughed. "I suppose I should have invested in airplanes, then."

"Interesting." So old money. *Called it.* I almost sent Lexi a quick text to boast about my powers of deduction, only that would have been unprofessional and I was anything but unprofessional.

The road looped back and forth as we climbed even further upwards. Cresting a rise, I caught a glimpse of the LA skyline in the near distance. It was both more beautiful and more muggy than I'd remembered it being.

"It's coming up here on the left," Dean shouted over the wind.

We passed a small grove of madrone trees and came upon a house. If you could truly call something that large a house. The Victorian monstrosity seemed out of place in the neighborhood. It was at least a hundred years older than the rest of the houses on the block, which were all slightly different configurations of glass and steel.

"Wow."

Dean pulled into the long, pristine circular driveway and parked. "I know. It's a marvel to see in LA, right? Not many Victorians left anymore."

The age of the house was making me question how well the security system had been wired. How easy would it have been to disable?

Dean hopped out of the car—which apparently was his thing—and waited for me beside the front steps. "Uh..."

"What?" I noticed it as soon as I asked the question. The large oak front door was cracked open. Not enough to notice from the street, but enough to see from the porch.

I pulled myself together and pointed at Dean. "You stay here by your car, I'm going to run around the back. I assume there's a back entrance?"

He nodded. "Several."

I looked him in the eye. "*Stay here.*" That was the last thing I needed, a client getting hurt on a job because I gave in to his annoying, odd requests.

I took a final glance at him with his arms crossed over his chest before ducking around the side of the house. The wrought iron gate was unlatched. Clearly we weren't dealing with a criminal mastermind here. A professional would never make these kinds of simple mistakes.

I didn't usually carry a firearm, but I was itching for my trusty taser, Tasha. Tasha had taken down quite a number of men twice my size. I avoided fighting as much as possible, however, husbands who had been caught in the act were glad to leave their opinion of me on my face in the form of a black eye. A definite downside of the job. Malcolm used to always tell me I needed to learn how to fight for the day that Tasha wasn't enough. Luckily, that day hadn't come yet.

The side garden was immaculately pruned and plucked with a shaded cabana overhead blocking out the already warm California sun. Cement steps led down a walkway to the sloped backyard. A large terraced porch made up the back of the house with floor to ceiling windows covered by gauzy white drapes. All the doors were closed. I stopped and watched for movement, my heart beating fast in my chest. I hadn't been expecting an active burglary during an ongoing theft investigation. I guessed I should have expected the unexpected. There, the curtains shifted—someone was inside. I climbed the steps carefully and poised my hand over the handle, slowly testing to see if it was unlocked. It was.

Crash!

A solid body pushed through the door, knocking me to the ground. Pain bloomed in my hip and shoulder. I tried to turn and catch a quick glimpse of the perpetrator, only the side of my head had smacked into the stone terrace, temporarily disarming me. By the time I'd recovered and gotten to my feet there was no sign of them. *"Dammit."* I rubbed my temple, praying I didn't have a concussion, and opened the door with my other hand. It had all happened so fast it was hard to make out any discernible details. The dark figure hadn't seemed to be carrying anything with them, at least nothing large. Had Dean been robbed *again*? It seemed impossible. Two times in twenty-four hours.

The room I entered was pitch dark. I felt around for a light switch and flicked it on. I was in some kind of den with dark green plush furniture askew around the space and tapestries hung on the wall. I doubted Mr. Prescott's uncle kept it like that normally. *Someone* had clearly been messing around in here.

"Uh, Mr. Sun?" Dean called from somewhere farther inside the house.

Dammit, I'd told him to stay outside. He was starting to be a real problem. I should have never agreed to let him come along.

I followed his voice through the doorway, down a long series of hallways of dark wood, and into a grand foyer with marble floors and a glass chandelier that hung from a three-story-high ceiling.

Dean stood right past the front door, a body in front of him on the marble.

"What the hell?" I raced over to meet him, narrowly avoiding the growing pool of dark red blood. "I gotta call this in." I whipped out my phone to get ahold of the cops.

"Should we do CPR or something?" Dean asked in earnest, his body language more relaxed than I would have expected for someone who had just found a dead person in their home.

"Unfortunately, you have to have *blood* in your body to perform CPR," I said calmly, referencing the body-sized pool of red under the man's frame.

He crossed his arms. "*Well shit.*"

"Do you recognize him?" I asked. The guy was about forty, balding, heavy set, and tall. Small, deep wounds littered his front. Probably made by some kind of pocket knife judging by the size of the cuts.

Dean shook his head. "No."

Seeing that he didn't need immediate support, I focused my attention on the phone and relayed any information I could to the police. They were sending someone over immediately.

When I turned back toward the body Dean was crouched down, examining it. "What are you doing? *Don't touch anything.*"

He snapped up and held out his hands, his eyes wide. "I didn't. I was just checking something."

40

What was this guy doing? "*Checking something?*"

He shrugged. "Yeah, he's got pretty nice clothes for a thief, that's all."

I studied the body and reluctantly agreed. For such a sloppy criminal he was dressed in expensive designer labels. Maybe he *wasn't* our thief at all. "Someone knocked me down on my way in. *They're* probably our culprit."

He caught my gaze. "Are you okay?"

He'd found a dead body in his home and he was asking *me* if I was okay? "I'm fine, Mr. Prescott. It's gonna take a lot more than a hard knock to take me out."

"I don't suppose you saw their face, did you?"

I shook my head.

"*Damn.*"

"This is turning out to be a very strange case, Mr. Prescott. Are you sure there's nothing that you've failed to mention to me?"

He pinched his brows together and frowned. "Like what, exactly?" he said, his tone cooling.

I crossed my arms. "I don't know. I'm confused, is all."

"That makes two of us, then."

I motioned towards the victim. "Can you...stand here with the body until the police arrive?"

"*Why?*" His eyes widened. "What are you going to do?"

I gestured behind me. "Some furniture was turned over and out of place when I walked through. I have a sneaking suspicion it's worse in the rest of the house."

"Shit, really?" He took a couple steps back and ground his teeth.

Now I had his attention. Was the state of the house more alarming to him than a murder? This guy was a mystery all on his own.

"Yes, so *stay here.*"

He caught my gaze. "Wait, do you think whoever knocked you over earlier will be coming back?" he asked, his lips pressed together in a wary expression.

"Do you...want to come with me?" I offered. Maybe he was more worried than I'd first realized.

He looked at the door and then down at the body. "No, I'm okay. You go look around. There might be someone else in the house, right?"

I nodded. "It's a large house. They'd probably need a sizable crew to cover the place quickly."

He crossed his arms over his chest again and straightened his frame. "Okay, be safe."

Be safe? "I'm always safe, Mr. Prescott." That wasn't typically true, but I wanted to reassure him for some reason I couldn't identify. Maybe it was seeing his usually intense dark eyes go dim, or the front he was obviously putting on for my benefit.

I slipped out of the foyer and down the hall that led to a massive main room with a dormant fireplace, Turkish carpet covered wooden floors, and plush furniture strewn about. Chairs were knocked over, heavy bottom glasses were shattered, and books were thrown from their shelves to the floor. This wasn't the typical scene of a robbery. Someone had been looking for something specific. Clearly they'd had trouble finding it. Question is, did they locate what they were looking for in the end? Whoever had barreled past me hadn't been carrying anything with them, though maybe the object was small. Jewels? Papers? The rich had an assortment of stealable items.

God, this case was already so frustrating. Why steal a priceless statue one night and then come back in the morning to steal something else? Could it be two separate cases of thievery? One right after the other, unrelated? It seemed pretty improbable, though I'd learned early on that life was often crazier than it appeared at first glance.

I walked through the room across from the main lounge, which had also clearly been ransacked—more overturned furniture, more broken glass, and tarnished books. Whoever had been rummaging around must have been here for quite a while without any luck.

I retraced my steps when I began to hear the sirens nearing. Dean stood a few feet from the body, his eyes fixed on the floor. He'd closed the front door behind him. "You okay?" I asked.

He jerked his head up and gave me a strained smile that didn't reach his eyes. "Yep, I'm swell. Did you find anything interesting?"

"It's what I thought, I'm sorry to say. The rest of the house has been turned over and searched through. Do you have any idea what they could have been looking for?"

Dean rubbed his temple with his hand. "I honestly have no idea. My uncle collects many objects and artifacts. It could be anything."

"I'm afraid now that this case involves a murder you might not have much choice in telling your uncle."

He went still, the color draining from his face. "He's gonna kill me."

I didn't know how to respond to that. I wasn't what many would call *comforting*. "Hopefully things will pan out quickly and we can have it wrapped up before your uncle comes back. When did you say he was returning?"

He took a long time to answer as if just noticing I'd asked him a question. "Two weeks."

The sirens stalled as they reached the house and a heavy fist banged on the front door. "Police!"

Two uniformed officers I didn't recognize entered and immediately started marking off the area. I gave them my information, my detective license, and my history with the case so far. Dean seemed to be pretty uncomfortable answering the cop's questions, crossing his arms and talking slowly in a low tone. It was almost as if he was more tense around the police than he had been with the dead body. He kept puzzling me further and further. What was this guy's deal?

FOUR

About ten or so minutes later another two cars arrived up the drive. I walked down to greet them as a man got out of the driver's side of a black, police-issued sedan.

Ah great. "Detective Warner, so lovely to see that you're still working homicide." Of course it would have to be him.

Detective Warner, a stern-faced blond man in his thirties seemed surprised to see me. "Mr. Sun. How did you manage to get yourself wrapped up in a murder? I thought you usually stuck to panty snatchers and bigamists?"

I smiled, though there was no friendliness in the gesture. "That's why I called you, isn't it? LA's *finest*?" I made sure to add as much sarcasm and disdain as I could on the last phrase. Detective Warner was an asshat and never hesitated to remind me how much he disliked private detectives when we brushed paths. Which had been many times over the years. In fact, he'd been there for one of my first ever cases, back when I had a more optimistic view of the world and assumed—silly me—that a detective would want to help me solve my case if it meant taking a dangerous criminal off the streets. I wouldn't be making that mistake again.

He narrowed his eyes and looked around. "What happened to your partner? Isn't your little gig usually a duo act?"

Bastard.

"I'm alone," I said simply, trying to avoid the topic at all costs.

He smiled. "And so you are." Warner walked past me with his partner Detective Caruso trailing behind, who ignored me entirely. "Who owns the house?" Warner asked as we walked up the front steps.

I let out a silent breath and forced myself to be professional. "My client's uncle, a Mr. Williams. He's vacationing in Greece at the moment."

We reentered through the front door. Dean was still speaking in hushed tones to a uniformed officer, but stopped as we walked into the foyer.

"Detectives, my client, Mr. Prescott," I introduced them, though they didn't seem particularly interested in being acquainted. Even Dean's usual Crest smile was nowhere to be seen.

Warner glanced down at the body on the floor. "Who's the stiff?" He looked to me for an answer and I gave him my most unhelpful shrug. He turned to the closest police officer instead.

"Don't know, detectives. He didn't have ID on him and no wallet or keys. Either he was packing light or the second perp took it with him."

"Second perp?" Detective Caruso asked.

I let the officer fill them in on my statement, feeling no need to help more than I was obligated.

"*Huh*, strange." Warner turned his attention back to Dean. "Do you know this guy, Mr. Scott?"

"It's uh, Prescott, and no, I don't. Never seen him before in my life."

"So you don't know why he'd be found dead, and of all places, here, on your uncle's marble floor?"

Dean crossed his arms and shifted his stance. "No idea at all."

"*Hmm.*" Warner inspected the body, noticing all the small stab wounds I had. "About ten or so wounds here, pretty erratic. Clearly a newbie."

I snorted into my fist.

He glared back at me. "Something to tell the class, Sun?"

Fine, I'd throw the asshole a bone, even though he didn't deserve it. "Five of those wounds are placed perfectly over the heart and two major arteries. The other wounds were likely made to mask the precision of the previous. Nothing erratic to me."

Warner widened his grin, his eyes darkening. "*Thanks.* Now that you've given your statement I'm sure you have other cheating scandals to work on. Don't let us keep you, Mr. Sun."

I returned his grin and clapped my hands together. "Fine by me, I'd like a word with my client. Mr. Prescott?"

Dean seemed equally eager to leave, his eyebrows raising.

"I'm afraid we're not quite done with Mr. Prescott," Warner interjected, rising to his feet again. "We'll need to ask him a few more questions."

"Which you can do later down at the station, I'm sure," I said, knowing full well it was the truth.

Warner gritted his teeth. "Fine, just stay close by, Mr. Prescott. We'll need to contact your uncle too, so if you could give one of the officers his information that would be appreciated."

Dean forced a smile. "Will do."

He followed me out the front door to the drive where he released a long held breath.

"You okay?" I asked. He seemed more flustered now that he was away from all the cops, like he'd been holding in his nerves.

He shook his head and smiled. "Fine. What about you? It seemed like you knew those guys."

I scoffed. "Yep, we've met a few times. Not to be bleak, but I don't hold much confidence in those chuckleheads to solve this case."

We stopped by the fountain in the middle of the circular driveway, far from the ears of the officers milling around outside the front of the house. The morning smog had lifted and the noon sun beat down on our shoulders. The warmth was nice after the coldness of the darkened house.

Dean turned to me. "Are you...firing me as a client?" he asked carefully in a low tone.

"What?" It caught me off guard. I hadn't even thought about it. I'd never abandoned a case before—even when I probably should have.

He stammered on. "I get it, this was just supposed to be a simple theft job and now that murder is involved you want to stay as far away as possible."

"That's not—"

"No, I get it. I would do the same thing. But the thing is, I *need* you, Mr. Sun. Now more than ever. I'll even double your fee if you can get to the bottom of this before my uncle gets back. *Please.*" He clasped his hands in front of him, his face contorted with distress.

Should I drop the case? It was true that I didn't typically take on murder or suspicious death cases unless the situation and the price was right. *Double my fee, huh?* It wasn't only the fact that I couldn't afford to quit this case, it was also that I knew if I didn't solve it Detective Warner and his little sidekick would make a total mess of the situation, no doubt throwing a key piece of evidence under the rug or ignoring a major point of investigation—as I'd witnessed on more than one occasion. I trusted those two about as far as I could throw them—which considering Caruso's beer gut, wasn't very far.

However, something about this case still felt...off. Was I going to take the risk that Dean was telling me the full truth and that this wasn't all going to blow back in my face later? He seemed like a nice guy, however his carefully crafted socialite veneer was already starting to wear thin from the stress. Could I trust him?

I rubbed my bare finger where I was used to the feeling of a ring, a habit I hadn't quite gotten rid of yet. Dean smiled pitifully, his brows pinched together low over his eyes.

There was something about him that interested me. Maybe it was because he was handsome or because he was so confident, but there was something there that made me want to help him. He didn't have many other options. Most other agencies would turn him down now that a murder was involved and now that the police were trying to take over the investigation. I was all he had. His only option.

I let out a deep sigh, already planning for the worst. "Okay, but if I'm going to continue with this case I need full transparency from you, Mr. Prescott."

He bobbed his head eagerly. "Of course."

I tried to appear stern, hardening my features. "This is serious. No messing around."

He grinned a lopsided, schoolboy smile. "Deal."

Not very reassuring.

Now where to start on this shit show. "Okay, I guess let's pick up your friend and head back to my office. Did you call her?"

"Yeah, she'll be ready." He hopped into the car and waited for me to open the passenger door and slide in. "Also, you can call me Dean, detective. Mr. Prescott was my father."

"Okay, well we need to get a move on, Dean. The more time we waste the more time Detective Warner has to misinterpret evidence."

"You got it." He turned over the engine and slammed the gas pedal to the floor, moving us away from the house and down the winding roads of the LA hills.

Careful what you wish for, Noah.

FIVE

Dean pulled up in front of a luxury high-rise near downtown, all glass and steel. It took only a minute before the doorman opened the door for an equally luxurious looking woman. An emerald dress hung loosely from her lithe frame; it ruffled in the soft breeze.

"Dean, darling, how are you holding up?" she asked in a smooth, calming tone as she walked over. When she reached the car she took off her dramatically large, no doubt expensive, sunglasses. She had beautifully pale green eyes, cool almond skin, and a curly mass of golden hair up in a bun at the top of her head.

"I'm...okay. Felicity, this is the detective I was telling you about, Mr. Sun."

She smiled and waved. "Hello, detective."

I nodded in her direction. "Nice to meet you."

Dean got out of the car and kissed her on the cheek before pulling his seat back so that Felicity could sit behind us.

They seemed oddly close for friends—familiar. Was Felicity his girlfriend? But then why not simply say that? Rich people always seemed to have strange boundaries with friends and partners. Maybe *that* was what I was picking up on.

I was curious to ask her a few prodding questions on the way back to the office, however it was hard to hear anything over the wind as we whipped past downtown to the east side.

Dean parked the car and I led them up the stairs to the office. They both seemed out of place in their nice clothes, like they were on their way to a charity brunch or whatever rich people got up to on a Saturday afternoon.

Lexi was back behind the front desk, typing away at her laptop. She looked up with an arched brow—no doubt wondering why we'd been gone for so long. I hadn't bothered to text her because I knew it would only cause her to worry. She was a worrier, even if she was good at masking it.

"Long story. I'll fill you in," I said as our group passed her desk. She got up and followed us into my office. Dean gave up the only seat for his friend to sit.

"I can grab a second chair," I offered.

He shook his head and crossed his arms. "No, that's okay. I think I'll stand."

"Okay then." I sat behind my desk and Lexi returned to her corner beside me, her laptop open and ready to go.

"Lexi, this is Dean's friend, Felicity. Felicity, this is Lexi. She helps me out on cases sometimes."

"Hi," Lexi said without looking up from her screen.

"Nice to meet you." Felicity raised her eyebrow and then sat back in her chair.

"So, obviously this...murder complicates things," I started.

Lexi bumped my arm under the table. "*Murder?*"

I sighed. "Yes, this case just got upgraded from organized robbery to murder."

I explained how the house had been ransacked, some key details from what I remembered of the crime scene, and about the victim, all while Lexi typed furiously.

She turned to Dean. "You just have shit luck, don't you?"

"*Lexi,*" I chided her. She had a bad habit of saying everything she thought out loud.

55

He smiled. "Apparently, kid, yeah."

She frowned. "I'm not a kid."

"Oh?" He raised an eyebrow and smiled.

Yeah, Lexi was fifteen going on thirty, though she was more fragile than she seemed. Strangers couldn't see past her snappy, sarcastic personality like I could.

Felicity glanced back at Dean and they appeared to have a tense, silent conversation. So he hadn't told her about the dead guy either. *Interesting.*

I cleared my throat. "Yes, this is now a murder and we need to solve it quickly because the cops are biting at our tails."

"Warner?" Lexi asked.

I nodded. "Yep."

"*Prick*," she mumbled under her breath, which made me grin.

"I think our first course of action needs to be nailing down our suspect list and then I can contact some of my art fences to see if anyone knows anything about the statue. I think for now at least we can assume that the two crimes are linked, the murder and the theft. We just need to figure out how." I was expecting some quippy interjection from Dean, only he was oddly silent. I looked up to catch his eye.

"So...I, um. I might have done a thing," Dean said from the back wall where he was leaning by the door.

"Done a thing?" I asked, confused by his body language.

He walked over and dropped a piece of fabric onto the desk in front of me that he'd taken from his suit jacket pocket.

"What is this?"

He flushed. "I grabbed it from the dead guy's hand."

My jaw dropped and I snapped it shut just as fast. "You *what*?"

"He was clutching it in his fist," he said as way of an explanation.

Not good enough.

"You took this from the body? Didn't I tell you not to touch anything?" Was this guy *trying* to get arrested? I restrained myself and took in a slow breath to calm down.

He shrugged, his cheeks a warm shade of pink. "I thought it could help you catch whoever did this."

Felicity seemed embarrassed by her friend, with an awkward, pinched expression on her face, like she was used to his antics.

I narrowed my eyes and let out a heavy sigh. "It could also get us both arrested for tampering with a crime scene, Mr. Prescott. If the cops knew you'd taken that they would be more than pissed. Warner would have your head, for sure."

He crossed his arms and bit his lip. "Oh."

At least he had the *decency* to look guilty.

Lexi leaned over the desk and glanced at the scrap of fabric. "A suit jacket?"

I gave Dean a withering look before switching my focus to the evidence. The fabric was coarse and threaded with different shades of gray. Most likely wool. "Maybe."

"So he grabbed the killer and tore off some fabric in their struggle?" Dean said quickly, as if asking for permission to add to the conversation.

"*Possibly.*"

"He must have been pretty strong to pull off a piece of someone's clothing," Felicity added. "That's hard to do."

I nodded in agreement. "Adrenaline gives you the strength to do some crazy things."

"Like mothers who lift cars off of their children?" Felicity offered.

"Yeah, something like that." I pulled out a pair of tweezers from the top drawer of my desk and placed the scrap of gray fabric into a small, clear evidence bag. "Though I'm not sure how this will help me at all. It would be almost impossible to connect a piece of fabric to a person."

Dean frowned. "Why not?" he asked like a petulant child.

Was he serious? "Do you realize how many articles of clothing are made every year, Mr. Prescott? *Billions.*"

"This isn't any old fabric, though," he argued.

I waved my hand. "Pray tell."

"It's expensive. Your secretary was right, it's probably suiting material."

Lexi smiled, though it didn't reach her eyes. "I'm not his secretary."

He raised an eyebrow. "Oh, then...what are you?"

She counted off on her fingers. "Head research, booking, administrative assistant, accountant, everything he doesn't want to do."

Felicity smiled.

"*Okay*. Sorry," Dean continued. "My point is that this fabric probably comes from an expensive suit shop. It's not some random fabric. And another thing."

"Another thing?" I asked.

He nodded his chin towards the scrap. "It smells."

"It *smells*?" What the hell was this guy on about?

"The cologne, it smells expensive. That's another lead."

I held the open evidence bag near my face and took a whiff. "I wouldn't exactly call that a lead, Mr. Prescott. Are you saying you now want me to track a murderer down by the scent of his cologne?"

Dean leaned down by the chair Felicity was sitting in. "Why can't you?" he asked, as if it was a totally normal and logical practice.

I studied the evidence bag with the scrap of fabric inside and let out a heavy breath. "I think we're straying from the point here. Let's get back to the party. That would be a much more fruitful line of discussion."

"Fine. So you said that you think the two crimes are connected, right?" Dean asked.

"Maybe, maybe not, either way it's the best place to start, so we'll assume they are for now." I turned to Felicity. "So, Mr. Prescott was telling us that you were there Friday night and that you could help us identify some of the other party guests?"

She smiled. "Yes, I made a list.

Dean frowned and returned to his spot against the back wall. I supposed I'd offended him by ignoring his silly inquiry.

Lexi started typing as Felicity read down the list. We skipped the ones that Lexi had already found from Dean's recollections—Mr. Hackney and Mrs. Wong.

"And then there was Tyler Conrad. He's a playboy. I connected with him at a mutual acquaintance's party and he expressed interest in coming to the event to talk about our business opportunity."

Lexi snapped her fingers. "*Tyler* Conrad. That makes sense."

"You know him?" I asked.

"Tyler Conrad is LA royalty," she explained. "Both his father and grandfather were in the film business. They made a lot of money during the Hollywood golden age."

"Interesting." I hummed and looked back toward the pair. "So this business opportunity, what line of work are you two in exactly, Mr. Prescott?"

He cleared his throat and gestured with one hand. "Import/export, mostly."

How vague.

"Huh, and that seems to have attracted quite an odd set of guests." I had hoped to bait him or Felicity into giving me more, into giving away whatever secret they were hiding, but their expressions didn't change.

"I suppose you could say that," Felicity replied.

I moved on. "And who else was at this party?"

Felicity checked the list on her phone. "Everly Sanderson."

"And what's her story?" I asked.

"I believe she was looking for some investors to start a new makeup line. Honestly, I didn't talk with her long. There was a lot going on that night," she replied. "Did you speak with her, Dean?"

Dean shook his head. "Briefly when she arrived, but she was occupied with one of the other guys most of the night. I can't remember who, maybe that real estate kid."

"Mr. Gomez?" I confirmed.

He shrugged. "Sure."

"Okay." I nodded.

Lexi typed all that information into her notes. She'd also added a basic drag and drop timeline to the top of the page. Smart thinking.

"So this party started around...when?" I asked.

Felicity mused. "*Hmm.* It was scheduled for ten, however the first guest arrived at around ten thirty."

I nodded. "And who was that first guest?"

"Mr. Hackney," Dean interjected. "I remember because he brought a case of those awful cigars as a gift and it stunk up the place."

"Okay, and when did the event end?"

Dean looked over at Felicity to confirm. "I want to say around two thirty in the morning? Though the caterers left right before two."

"They didn't stay to clean up?" I asked.

"No, I had already hired cleaners to come the next day, though of course I canceled that as soon as I realized the statue was missing. I locked the place up tight and searched around for some help. That's when I found you online."

I turned to Felicity. "And when did *you* leave? Were you there the whole time?"

She widened her eyes. "I—yes, what are you asking, exactly?"

I shrugged. "I'm simply confirming your actions that night."

Dean walked over again to the desk to loom above me. "Felicity is my oldest and dearest friend. She's *family*," he said firmly. "I don't want you wasting time looking into her, only the guests."

I raised my hands. "I was not implying anything at all. I need to know where everyone was at certain times. It's standard procedure. I'm sorry if I offended you, Mrs..."

"Miss Reed. But you can call me Felicity, Mr. Sun. And you haven't offended me. I understand you have a process." She laced her fingers together across her knee. "I was at Dean's place from eight until after two-thirty when he noticed the statue was missing. We were both there the whole night. And from what I can remember, nobody left the party or was missing for any large chunk of time. Of course we were both preoccupied entertaining our guests, so I can't be *completely* certain. It's hard to keep track of everyone."

"I see. Thank you for your candor, Felicity." I turned to Dean. "So when did the caterers arrive?"

"I think around eight thirty or nine."

"Nine," Felicity confirmed.

"And you can say without a doubt that the statue was there at nine?"

He furrowed his brows. "Yes, I can."

"Okay."

We went through the rest of Felicity's guest list and Lexi started on some light research to add to her case notes. Dean stood in the back of the office sulking for most of it, pouting his full lips and crossing his arms. It almost made me cave on his stupid cologne idea. *Almost.*

"So in all there were nine strangers in your house, plus the two of you," I confirmed.

"I guess that sounds right," Dean mused.

"That's a pretty small pool of suspects. Which is good because we need to act fast." I checked my watch. It was almost one o'clock in the afternoon. "I'll start tracking people down and interviewing them today and see where that gets us. I should have some kind of update by tomorrow."

Dean frowned and shifted his stance. "I was kind of hoping that I could tag along for the interviews."

Tag along? "Clients don't usually come with me for interviews," I explained. That was the last thing I needed. I worked best alone. "You should go home."

"You mean to a murder scene?"

"Well—" I faltered.

"You can always stay with me, darling, if you don't want to be alone. You know that, Dean," Felicity offered.

I grinned. "There, problem solved."

He waved his hand through the air. "Problem *not* solved. How am I supposed to relax while I know a murderous thief is running around? You said it yourself, time is limited. Besides, you'll need me."

"I'll *need* you?" I hated to burst his rich-boy bubble, but I didn't *need* anyone. Most of all *him*. This was my job, and I was damn good at it. I didn't need someone butting in and messing everything up.

He went on, "Do you think any of these people are going to talk to a private detective? They'll slam the door in your face. You need an in. Plus, they'll speak more freely if someone from their own social circle is the one asking the questions."

Lexi hummed. "He has a point."

"Does he, though?" I mumbled.

He held up his hands. "I promise I'll take the backseat. You won't even notice I'm there."

I found that extremely hard to believe. I closed my eyes and let out a breath, weighing my options. "I think this is a terrible idea. Unfortunately, we don't have the time to argue about it." He could ride along, but we were't partners. He was there as a courtesy, nothing more.

Dean grinned, revealing straight white teeth.

I told myself that if he was any less attractive I would have said *absolutely not*, but I knew that was a lie. Something about Dean pissed me off while simultaneously drawing me in. He intrigued me, and curiosity was a weakness of mine.

You know what they say, Noah, *curiosity killed the cat*. Let's just hope I didn't end up like the cat.

SIX

Dean insisted on driving again, and against my better judgement, I let him. Maybe there was something to the idea that all these rich people would feel more comfortable around one of their own, and Dean's car probably cost about ten times more than my hand-me-down nineties Jeep.

However, that feeling faded fast as Dean turned the wrong way towards the Beverly Hills strip. "Where are you going?" I asked. "The catering company is south of here."

He grinned and patted my knee. "Don't look so uptight, detective. We'll get there eventually."

"I thought you were the one concerned about solving this case before your uncle came back?"

"I am." He flicked his hand through the air. "We're just making a quick pit stop along the way."

I wouldn't call driving in the opposite direction *on the way*, however I was getting tired of arguing with him. It seemed like he had an extra store of energy saved up just for annoying me. If he wanted to waste time, it was his money. I needed another coffee. A large one.

I was fairly familiar with Beverly Hills. Many of my cases took me over to this side of Los Angeles. The strip was busy this afternoon as it was most afternoons. Dean sped forward and secured a tight parking spot along the curb—a spot many in their huge Escalades and F150's couldn't dream of fitting in.

"So what exactly are we doing here?" My question was answered for me as I glanced up at the name of the shop in front of us—Parisian Fragrance Exchange. Right, his silly idea about the cologne.

Dean hopped out of the car and wandered over to the sidewalk. "I know you think this is a waste of time, only I don't. I think if we can match that scrap of fabric to one of these colognes we'll be one step closer to figuring out who this guy was."

"How would that help us, exactly?" I was less than excited as I got out of the car and followed Dean into the shop. An electronic chime rang to let the shop owners know we'd entered.

Dean went on, "Well a fragrance says a lot about a person."

"Does it? What if he didn't pick it out himself? What if his wife bought it for him for their anniversary and he hates it but didn't want to hurt her feelings?"

He frowned, narrowing his eyes at me. "You're ruining it."

I smirked. "It's called detective work, Dean. Not imaginative play. Let's get this over with."

We wandered into the men's section and Dean began opening bottles and sniffing. I didn't know how he could remember what that scrap of evidence smelled like after all those samples, however he seemed determined, his features locked in concentration.

"Can I help you gentlemen find something?" a thick British accent asked.

Dean set down his latest bottle and turned. "Ah, yes please," Dean replied in a pretty compelling British accent of his own. "We're in a spot of bother,"

The older salesman seemed thrilled to find a fellow countryman.

"I'm Charles, and this is my brother-in-law, Nick," Dean introduced us. "Nick is married to my brother James, and next week is their anniversary."

The clerk smiled. "I see."

"Yes, and the trouble is Nick bought my brother a fragrance a few years ago when they were dating and wants to purchase the same one as his anniversary gift, only he can't seem to remember which one he bought last time."

"Oh, do you remember anything about the bottle?" The clerk's brow furrowed.

I was a little annoyed to have to play along with this act of his, but I couldn't contradict him now without embarrassing myself further. "I have a terrible memory and James already threw away the old bottle."

"Yes," Dean added. "Which is why we took a scrap of one of James' old shirts in hopes that we could match it by the scent."

"*Really?*" The clerk's eyebrows shot up. We were definitely his most interesting customers of the day, if not the year.

I handed Dean the evidence bag and he opened it for the clerk to smell. He scrunched up his nose in concentration and looked around the store. "Musky, lots of leather, and top notes of tobacco." He walked to a section in the back with small bottles of dark glass. "I can't quite place it; I feel like I've smelled it before." He picked up a bottle, then set it down for another.

"Yes, it's got that rather old fashioned fragrance to it, doesn't it?" Dean asked. I stood behind while Dean and the salesman sampled different bottles. After another ten minutes the clerk shook his head. "I'm sorry, gentlemen, I'm not sure I can match that fragrance *exactly*. These two are probably the closest, but I don't think they're the exact same." He referenced two bottles to his right.

"Well, thank you for trying. I think we'll keep looking. Maybe something will jog Nick's memory and we can try again."

The salesman seemed genuinely saddened that he hadn't been able to help us, and I was momentarily guilty. Until I remembered that I was *not* Nick married to James, and I was going to have a *strong* word with Dean about dragging me into his storytelling.

"I'll meet you at the car, Nick," Dean said with a quick glance my way. That was fine with me. I was eager to get out of there and back to doing some *real* detective work. Like *interviewing suspects*, for instance.

I climbed into the passenger seat and waited, watching throngs of tourists walking down the famous Rodeo Drive.

Dean came out a few minutes later and jumped back in the driver's seat. "That was a bust," I said, stating the obvious only to drive home my point. I was *right* and he was *wrong*.

He hummed. "Maybe." He put on his seatbelt and turned over the engine. "Here, for you." He handed me a small gray gift bag, inside was a black bottle shaped in an oblong rectangle.

"You bought me cologne?" I'd never had a client buy me a personal gift before. I didn't know how to feel about it.

"I felt kinda bad that we wasted so much of that guy's time. He really bought our sob story."

I snorted. "I think you mean *your* sob story. What was all that? The accent? The on the spot character names?"

70

He shrugged and said, "I was into theater in high school." As if that explained it all.

"Well did I have to be married to James?"

He looked over, a line creasing between his brows. "Do you have a problem being married to a James? It was just a story, detective."

"I-I know that." Was it obvious to him that I was gay? Or had he plucked the story out of the air? I'd been told by many in my life that I didn't *seem* gay. Whatever that meant.

"Besides, I thought this cologne matched your whole leather-jacket-private-eye vibe."

"Okay...thanks," I mumbled, rolling the bottle in my hand.

He turned away to look for traffic. "You're welcome."

The cologne was dark and musky with notes of vanilla and tobacco. I hadn't worn any fragrance in a while. I didn't see the point. Who was I impressing? The typical sort of clients that hired me didn't care and I had no love life to speak of. I normally wore whatever fragrance I'd been gifted that year for Christmas. Only, this year my Christmas gift had been getting dumped by my fiancé. Lucky me.

While Dean was concentrating on weaving back into traffic I sprayed a little of the cologne on my neck and pocketed the bottle. Once we were on the road I said, "*Now* can we interview the caterers?"

Dean smirked. "Yes, yes we can."

* * *

Rose Catering Company was a small operation out of Koreatown. The front of the building was blank besides a small sign on the window with their logo—a rose laid over a crossing fork and knife.

"How did you find this place?" I asked out of curiosity. It seemed an unlikely pick for someone of Dean's wealth and status.

"Felicity found them actually, online. We had another company all lined up, only they canceled last minute. Rose Catering was the first to get back to us."

Ah, that made more sense. And the fact that they were a random pick made them more interesting as suspects. If one of them were our thief that meant it was a crime of opportunity. Which wasn't likely given the level of security the house *supposedly* had.

We tried the front door. Locked. "Let's go around back," I suggested. "Someone must be here, the lights are on." The beige building was a boring square. The back was a mirror of the front, only *this* door had been propped open by an empty milk crate. "Bingo."

Dean tried to go in first and I stopped him with my outstretched arm. "Can you at least pretend that I'm the detective here? What if they have a weapon?"

He sighed. "Fine, after you. Get shot first."

"*Thank you.*" I entered and knocked on the metal door as we passed. "Hello? Anybody here?"

A short hallway led to an impressive galley-style kitchen. Someone was cooking something; the smell of braised meat wafted down the corridor. "Hello?" I tried again. All the lights were on and the kitchen was a mess. Vegetables took over counters, and containers of ingredients were laid out—some open and empty.

"Back there," Dean whispered, nodding his chin in the direction of the noise. There was a sizzling and a flash of orange light, however I still couldn't see *who* was behind the stove.

We moved in closer. I made sure to keep Dean behind me so he didn't do something stupid and unpredictable....again. I knew when I took his case that I was going to be doing a little bit of babysitting, only not *nearly* this much.

"Hello?" Dean called out.

The man behind the stove stepped around the corner, his eyes narrowed and a sharp chef's knife in his hand. "What are you doing in here?" he barked, his words clipped.

I took a step back and put my arm out in front of Dean's chest instinctively. *Shit*, I'd been mostly joking about someone having a weapon. "We just want to ask you a few questions."

The man squinted a little harder and seemed to finally recognize Dean. He smiled. "Oh, Mr. Prescott. Why didn't you say it was you?" He looked between the two of us. "I'm sorry, we've been having some trouble lately with the local kids breaking in here and making a mess. That's why we locked the front door." His eyes were glassy and his cheeks slightly flushed. Had he been drinking?

I gazed down at the knife still in his hand.

He followed my gaze and laughed before lowering it. "Sorry, old habits."

What was he going to do if it *was* the neighborhood kids? Stab them? "I'm Detective Sun, I want to ask you a few questions about the party you catered for Mr. Prescott last night."

He turned back to the stove and shook the sauté pan, causing a loud pop and sizzle. "What about it? Was it not satisfactory?"

"It's not about the food," Dean added.

I put out my hand to make him stop talking. If I let him lead he'd start us off on the wrong foot. "We want to know if you saw anyone in the hallway back by the kitchen at any time during the party." That was a good place to jump in. Benign.

He shook the pan again and then turned off the flame. "*Hmm*, I saw *a lot* of people during the party. Why do you want to know?"

What was the most delicate way of asking if somebody was a thief? "Someone went into the study where they weren't supposed to be and we want to know if you noticed anyone go in there between the start of the party and the time you left." It was a broad timeline; hopefully he remembered something.

"I did not leave the kitchen at all during the party except to use the restroom once or twice. It's my staff who you should be talking to," he said, waving his hand and screwing up his nose.

"Really? And can we talk to them?" I asked. "Are they here today?"

He gestured behind him. "They're somewhere around here. They're always wandering off when I need them. Even during the party last night they abandoned me. I should fire them both. Try the supply closet."

"The supply closet?" Dean asked.

"Around the corner." The chef turned his attention back to his dish.

"Okay then." We passed the stove and around the corner to the left. Along the wall was a closet with a wide door.

Dean turned to me with pinched brows.

"I don't know," I answered in reply to his unasked question. I knocked on the door which earned a startled yip from inside. "Hello?"

"Just a sec," a lower voice called.

After much longer than a few seconds the door opened. The closet was more of a pantry, lined with shelves of food with a section for take-out containers and catering supplies. A man and a woman stood inside both wearing a similar uniform—the woman's dark apron hanging half off her body. The man was tall with ruffled brown hair and a wrinkled white shirt. The woman was short and round with tight braids held up in a bun. I couldn't help but notice how her purple lipstick had stained his lips the same shade. "Are we interrupting something?" I asked casually, trying not to smile.

The man opened and closed his mouth before saying, "Nope, what can we help you with? Are you ordering catering?"

"I'll have what *they're* having," Dean whispered next to my ear, making me bristle.

I introduced myself to them and explained our situation again. "So we just want to know if you saw anyone walking around where they shouldn't have been and where you two were most of the night."

The tall man who the girl had called Trent looked instantly angry, his shoulders hunched up and his mouth twisted in a tight line. "Are you accusing us of stealing something?"

Dean cleared his throat. "Actually I believe he was very carefully *not* accusing you of stealing anything."

Very helpful, thank you, Dean.

"We're professionals," said the girl who'd introduced herself as Cherry.

"I don't doubt that, we only want to know where you guys were between midnight and two. We're asking everyone," I added to try and make it sound more fair.

They looked between each other. "Um," Cherry spoke up first. "Well by that time catering was mostly over. We brought out some more champagne and then took a break while Max started cleaning the kitchen."

"Okay, and can Max confirm that?" I asked.

Cherry shrugged. "If you hadn't noticed Max is usually inebriated. I don't know what he remembers and what he doesn't."

That confirmed what I'd already suspected myself. Max was dipping into his own supply.

"I see. And did you notice anyone else in the hallway during your *break*?"

Trent shook his head and Cherry replied, "We were sort of preoccupied at the time. We weren't wandering around watching the guest's every move."

Dean smirked. "My uncle's house does have quite roomy closets, doesn't it?"

Cherry blushed and Trent looked like he wanted to punch Dean's face in. I understood the impulse. "Okay, well, thank you for your time. We'll contact you if we have any other questions." I herded Dean down the hallway and back to the kitchen. "Interviewing 101, Dean, don't antagonize the suspects unless you need to."

He grinned. "Oh that felt *completely* necessary to me, detective."

I controlled the urge to roll my eyes as we walked over to where Max was plating a dish, piping a green sauce from a plastic bag. "I have a couple more questions."

He gazed up in surprise, as if he'd forgotten that we'd been there only ten minutes ago. "What is it?"

"Your staff told us that they took a break near the end of the party, can you confirm that?"

He chuckled. "Can I confirm that? Hell yeah, I can confirm that. Did they think they were being sneaky running off to that closet for over half an hour? If I didn't need the help so bad I'd have fired them months ago."

So he wasn't as forgetful as Cherry had thought.

"And can I ask what you were doing between the hours of eight and nine this morning?" Now that we'd covered the theft, there was still the pesky murder to investigate.

He shrugged. "I was here. We have a large catering order for a wedding in Malibu. We've been prepping all morning since six."

"So you can confirm that both your staff were here during eight and nine as well? No one left or took a break during that time?"

He blew out a fast breath. "A break? Do I look like I have time to take a break?" He pushed the finished plate aside and started piping sauce onto the next one, identical in every way.

"Okay, well, thank you for your time, we'll contact you if we have any more questions."

He waved his hand in lieu of a goodbye and continued to concentrate on his task.

Out in the parking lot I stopped and looked Dean in the eye. "What part of silently standing in the background didn't you understand?"

He frowned. "Don't be so upset, I was only helping."

"Were you?"

He passed me and jogged ahead towards the car.

That wasn't a total bust, but it didn't give us any great leads either. Cherry and Trent had been *occupied* when the statue was stolen and Max was probably too drunk by the end of the night to steal much of anything, much less perform a high-level heist. Unless of course his whole functional-drunk act was just that, an act. It did seem like he might have the knife skills to perform precision cuts like the ones of our murder victim if he was butchering meats all day. I pocketed those thoughts away in my mind and met Dean at the car.

"Where to next, detective?" He'd thrown on a pair of dark shades and was leaning casually with his arm hanging over the back of the leather seat like he was in a perfume commercial or something.

"Lexi texted me an address for that Gomez kid. In order of likelihood, I think he's our next best bet."

Dean flicked his hand. "Why?"

"Because he's young, and young people do stupid things."

"But why steal a statue if he doesn't need the money?"

I shrugged as I slipped into the passenger seat. "We'll find out. Start driving."

He laughed. "*Yes, sir.*"

I cringed. "I'm sorry, I didn't mean for that to sound so demanding." Something about him was starting to eat at my nerves.

He smirked as he started the car. "I didn't mind. I kinda liked it, actually."

Oh, boy. "Just...drive, please."

He took one long, final look at me before pulling onto the road.

SEVEN

Miguel Gomez: twenty-four, social media star, and real estate hotshot. Everything Lexi had found about him online made me dislike him. Miguel seemed like kind of a douchebag. Maybe I'd let Dean take the reins on this interview. Someone who spoke the same rich-boy secret language.

I looked over at Dean as he drove the Speedster across town into the hills. No, he was annoying for sure, but he wasn't a douchebag. Douchebags didn't have classy and intelligent female friends like Felicity. Douchebags didn't buy people gifts without expecting something in return. Dean was just rich and overconfident.

Lexi had found Miguel's house easily online. "He doesn't even try to hide the address. What an idiot." She'd sent me snapshots of the house from his social media. It was a modern glass and white-concrete compound large enough to house at least five families.

We only had to pass one security gate, and luckily for us Dean knew someone else in the same neighborhood, so getting in was easy, all it took was one text. *One good reason to keep him around, I guess.*

"Damn, that is *some* house." Dean pulled up into the long driveway and stopped at the closed security gate. "How are we getting in?"

"The old fashioned way. We ask." I got out of the car and walked over to the intercom. I buzzed and waited for someone to pick up on the other side. And waited. And waited. *Nothing.*

"Nobody home?" Dean called.

I shrugged. "Apparently not. I walked back toward the car and stood behind the gate. The house was immaculate, almost *too* clean. The front porch was spotless—no flower pots, no stray basketballs or pool noodles. Even the concrete seemed freshly washed with no tire marks or grease stains. Either Miguel was obsessively clean or...

"Watcha thinkin'?" Dean asked.

I got back in the car. "I'm thinking that someone's a liar." I texted Lexi my hunch.

L: On it, give me 10 minutes.

There was no way this was Miguel's real house. "Lexi's doing some digging. We'll have to wait a minute."

Dean nodded. "Okay."

It was quiet in the car. Up in the hills you could hardly hear the murmur of traffic down below. I tapped my fingers absentmindedly against the dash.

After a couple minutes of silence Dean asked, "So why a detective?"

I turned. "What?"

He went on, "I just mean, it's a pretty unusual career. What made you want to become a private detective?"

"*Uh.* I read a lot of the Hardy Boys growing up?"

He laughed through his nose. "That's it?"

I shrugged. Why did he want to know? "I like...figuring things out, figuring *people* out. I almost went to law school, but can you picture me wearing a stuffy suit in some courtroom?"

He looked me up and down. "No, I really can't. You could have become the first lawyer to wear a leather jacket and sweatpants combo to court, though."

I forgot that I'd never changed my pants; I cringed. "*Agh*, yeah, I probably should have changed before we left for interviews."

He smiled. "Nah, I like it. It's very James Dean meets gym bro."

I laughed. "I'm not like either of those things, fortunately." I pointed at his suit. "Do you dress like this all the time? That seems uncomfortable."

He pressed his lapels flat with his fingers. "I notice that when I dress nice I get more respect."

"Doesn't your credit card usually do that for you?" I'd meant for it to be a joke, though I caught myself sounding bitter.

"Well, uh...no, not really. Besides, I want to be respected, *not* coddled. Going to the club and having everyone know my name just because I have money doesn't feel as good as you'd think. I'd rather people know who I am because of...me."

"I'm sorry, that was a rude question." I shook my head. "I shouldn't have asked that."

He waved his hand. "I don't care, you can ask me anything. I'm an open book."

There was that underlying feeling again that Dean was hiding something, pulling me back to reality. My phone buzzed—Lexi.

"We got ourselves a new address."

"Really?" Dean asked in surprise.

"And you'll never guess what neighborhood it's in."

He gave me a lopsided grin. "Don't say mine."

I laughed, showing him the screen. "Actually...mine."

He pinched his brows together and started the car.

* * *

This house was much more humble. Judging by the silver minivan that sat in the driveway, Miguel didn't live by himself. The house was a two-story Craftsman, which was nice and well-kept, only it resided on the east side. Not the Beverly Hills mansion that he'd claimed online.

Dean parked along the curb and we strolled up the walkway to the front door. Chalk drawings lined the cement in blue and pink scribbles, evidence that kids lived nearby.

I let Dean knock on the door and we waited. When it cracked open Miguel looked us up and down in confusion until he recognized Dean. He tried to shut the door in our faces, and I stopped it with my foot. *Ow, asshole.* "We need to talk to you, Mr. Gomez."

"You got the wrong house."

"Oh I'd say we have the right house, Miguel. It only took two tries."

"Miguel?" a soft woman's voice called. "Who's at the door?"

"No one, Ma," he shouted back.

Once he realized we weren't leaving he sighed and let go of the door, letting it swing fully open. "Thank you." I pulled my foot back. That was going to bruise, no doubt.

"What do you want?" he asked quietly.

Straight to the point, then. "We want to talk about the party last night."

He shrugged and put his hands in his pockets. "I don't have any money, so whatever you're thinking, forget it."

Dean laughed. "I wasn't thinking that at all, but now that you mention it..."

I hit his chest to make him shut up. "We don't care about..." I waved my hand across the house behind him, "...this. We only want to know what you were doing at the party between approximately midnight and two."

He narrowed his eyes. "Are you a cop?"

"No, private investigator. Not a cop," I said, hoping that put him at ease. "So where were you?"

He sucked on his teeth. "How am I supposed to remember what I was doing between midnight and two? I was hammered."

"Yes, I remember," Dean added unhelpfully.

I gave him a stern look and then turned back to Miguel. "Do you at least remember who you were with at the time?" I asked. He had to know *something*.

He shrugged. "I was hanging with that Tyler guy, but he kept running off to talk to that hot chick."

"The hot chick?"

He smirked. "You know, the Black one."

"Charming," Dean whispered.

"Did you stay in the lounge the whole night?" I asked, trying to stay on topic.

He looked at the doorframe and then back up to me. "I went to the bathroom a couple times if that's what you mean."

It wasn't. "Did you see anyone wandering around in the hallways any of those times?"

He paused to think about it, shifting his stance in the doorway. "I can't remember. Tyler was back there once or twice and one of the girls too."

"Which girl?"

He shrugged.

"Okay then, and what about this morning? What were you doing between eight and nine?"

"Why?"

"Just answer the question, please." I was trying to keep the whole murder thing under wraps for now. I didn't need the news spreading to any unknowing conspirators.

He shrugged. "I was here, I slept in."

"Okay, and can anyone confirm that?"

He started to speak.

"Other than your mother."

He rolled his eyes and took a second to think. "I talked to my neighbor when I was getting the mail this morning. He can prove that I didn't leave at all, ask him."

"We will. Thanks for your time, you've been *very* helpful." I tried not to sound bitter, though it probably didn't work. "We'll contact you if we have any further questions."

His face went stony and he squared off his stance, crossing his arms over his chest. "You're not going to tell anybody about this, right?"

I said, "About what?" just to annoy him.

He raised an eyebrow. "That I live here, bro."

"Why? Would it screw up your image if people knew you actually lived at home in the suburbs?" Dean asked.

He lowered his voice. "Man, this is my livelihood."

I rolled my eyes. "Calm down, Miguel. We won't be telling anyone anything. I don't care enough."

He straightened up and nodded in an effort to seem casual. "Cool."

We turned away from the house and got back in the car.

Dean let out a quick breath through his teeth. "Man, I knew that guy was a fake."

"You did?" I asked.

He nodded. "Behind that smile you could tell he reeked of desperation. Not to mention, you had to have noticed the fake watch and rented suit in his videos."

I *couldn't* say that. I hadn't. "Do you think he's desperate enough to steal a priceless statue, though? He doesn't seem that bad off, just... average."

"Yeah, only it's like you said. Young people are stupid and willing to do a lot to get ahead."

"I did say that, however I also don't know if Miguel is smart enough to pull off this level of heist. I doubt he even knows how security sensors work, much less how they're wired."

Dean smiled. "I think you underestimate the power of the internet, detective. You can learn anything nowadays. Besides, he works in real estate, surely he's walked through a ton of houses with complex security systems."

"*Hmm*, maybe. He's still on the list, but not at the top."

Dean nodded toward the neighboring house. "Are we going to check his alibi?"

I shook my head and laughed. "That was a bluff. I don't think Miguel killed anyone. The body had precise cuts, practiced cuts. Unless he's hiding a whole different backstory, he's not our killer, and I don't think he's that good of an actor."

"I suppose you're right." He started the car and put his shades back on. "Where to next?"

I glanced at my notepad. "That would be Mrs. Cassidy Wong."

Dean smirked. "Are you sure?"

Why was he looking at me like that? "Why?"

"We didn't make an appointment."

"Do we *need* an appointment?"

He turned and gave me a look that said he thought I was stupid. "She's a millionaire diamond mogul. Of course we need an appointment."

I smiled. "Well, I guess it's finally time for you to shine, Dean. You gotta use your connections and get us in to talk with her."

Dean sighed. "Fine, if I must." He pulled out his phone and started dialing—which worried me since he wasn't looking at the road. Whoever picked up on the other side must have been a close friend because Dean instantly grinned. "I've got an odd request, Pip. Are you up for the challenge?"

* * *

I didn't know who the hell Pip was, however when we reached the palatial mansion in Malibu the man at the gatehouse opened it for us on sight. Whatever strings Dean had pulled were pulled taut.

The house looked exactly like what I thought a diamond mogul's house would look like—ridiculously large, made of white stone, and heavily fortified with security. We passed a second gate to get into the main driveway from the private road that ran through a small park. This wasn't simply a house, it was an estate. I wondered idly how old the house was as we pulled up. Dean cut the engine and hopped out, handing his keys to a man standing close by in a royal blue vest.

I could hear the crashing of waves in the near distance. We must have been close to the water, though the view west of the drive was blocked by a maze of hedgerows. "Wow, she makes your uncle's house look casual."

Dean laughed through his nose. "Yeah, I believe Mrs. Wong inherited the house from her last husband who was in the gun trade, that on top of her own diamond dynasty surmounts to...this." He waved his hand across the landscape. "Also, if you see a peacock running around, don't go near it, they're surprisingly mean."

"Peacocks?" I asked.

He smirked. "Yeah, I wouldn't want one to peck out your eye, detective."

I frowned, imagining the prospect. "I wouldn't like that much either." We climbed the set of stairs up to the massive front door and it opened before we could knock. *Were you supposed to knock when they knew you were coming?*

An older man with a clean shaven face and a crop of finely-styled white hair answered the door. "Yes?" he asked, though it didn't sound like he wanted to hear the answer.

I let Dean answer for us.

He smiled brightly. "Dean Prescott and Mr. Sun for Mrs. Wong."

The housekeeper's—*butler's?*—eyebrows rose. "Regarding?"

Dean leaned in. "A sensitive personal matter."

That seemed to intrigue him. He nodded and opened the door wider. "Mrs. Wong is in her study. Follow me, gentlemen."

Once the housekeeper was far enough away I whispered, "That was easy enough."

Dean nodded. "You'd be surprised how boring working in a house this big can be. You only have to feed them a crumb of drama to get their attention." He smiled. "I didn't dare use the M word, though. That would have gotten us kicked out."

"Really?"

"Better to avoid scandal entirely at Mrs. Wong's level."

I wondered if she'd be turning away the police when they inevitably showed up at her door. That was, *if* Warner ever got this far.

We were led up a grand staircase to the second floor which wrapped around an open atrium—Italian manor style. The *study* happened to be more like a grand library. I was curious if Mrs. Wong had actually read any of the books or if they were also part of her inheritance.

"Dean Prescott and a Mr. Sun for you, ma'am," the housekeeper announced as we reached the threshold of the open doorway.

Mrs. Wong—a petite East-Asian woman in her sixties with a sleek bob of dark hair—was sitting behind a wooden desk that dwarfed her in size. Yet, she still commanded the room's full attention. She looked up and smiled. "Mr. Prescott, I wasn't expecting you today. Did you have another investment you wanted to discuss?"

Dean smiled politely. "Unfortunately, no. I've come about a different matter, something more serious."

There was a slight twitch at the corner of her lips as she managed to hold her composure. "Thank you, David, that will be all."

The housekeeper took the dismissal easily, though I could tell by his expression as he left that he'd wanted to stay and hear what the drama was all about.

Once the door was closed Mrs.Wong rose and came to greet us. "Let's sit over here." There was a small arrangement of sofas and chairs on the other side of the room beside an empty fireplace.

I chose a seat on a plush maroon sofa and Dean sat beside me, while Mrs. Wong chose the chair across from us. "Now, what is this really about?"

"Well, we've had a little mishap at my uncle's house," Dean started.

"What kind of mishap?" she asked earnestly.

"It seems that something valuable has been misplaced recently. *Very* recently."

"Ah." She nodded. "I see what you mean."

Dean turned to me. "This is Mr. Sun, he's a detective that I've hired to help find my lost item."

She glanced between the two of us. "And you think you *misplaced* this item during the party last night?"

He smiled. "Yes, that's where I was coming to. Obviously I don't think *you* had anything to do with it, we were just wondering if you saw anything suspicious last night that you could remember."

It wasn't so *obvious* to me, though why a woman as rich as her would want to steal the statue I didn't have a clue.

She nodded slowly and took a moment to think. "I do have *one* suggestion."

Dean opened his eyes a little wider, intrigued. "You do?"

"I would never mention this in polite company of course, but seeing as it's come to this," she motioned to me, "I feel as if it's my obligation to let you know."

Dean smiled politely. "I'm all ears."

"Something you might not know is that I've been acquainted with Tyler Conrad and his family since he was a child. My late husband was on the board of a company that Conrad's father ran. Honestly, it was a little bit of a shock to see him last night at your party, although he didn't react to me in the slightest. It's possible he doesn't remember me. The point I'm trying to get to is this: Tyler has a long history of being in places where things have disappeared, if you know what I mean."

Dean closed his eyes and nodded. "I understand completely."

"Yes, I gathered from his mother that it's been an ongoing issue since he was in high school." She lowered her voice. "This is *not* something I want getting out to the general public, mind you."

Dean mimed zipping his lips and throwing away the key.

"We have no interest in the press," I added.

Mrs. Wong turned as if just remembering I was there too. "Good. Because if it were to get out, well, I'd know who to trace it back to."

The threat was much less veiled than I'd expected from a socialite. I nodded in agreement to her unspoken terms.

She straightened her posture and smiled. "That's where I would suggest looking next, gentlemen. As for the party itself, I don't recall noticing anything all that strange. There was that burly fellow that kept making eyes at me which was a little odd, although if I remember correctly he didn't seem to stay the whole night. He left about halfway through the party if I remember correctly."

"Ah yes, I think I know who you mean," Dean replied. "He *was* a bit odd, wasn't he?"

I scribbled in my notebook.

Odd man?

Tyler Conrad?

"Thank you for your time, Mrs. Wong," I said. "I know it was on such short notice. If we have any further questions we'll contact you."

She smiled politely and rose from her chair. "I'm sure you will."

"Mrs. Wong, do you mind if I use your facilities before we leave?" Dean asked.

She waved her hand. "Of course not, it's down the hall to the left. David can help you if you get lost."

"Thank you." He took her hand and kissed it before we left the room. As soon as we exited the study and the door was shut Dean whispered, "Keep the old guy distracted, will you?"

"*What?*"

He didn't elaborate before running off down the hall, the *opposite* way that Mrs. Wong had directed.

Great, what the hell was he doing now? I waited in the open-air corridor for a minute before *slowly* walking down the stairs. The housekeeper, David, spotted me immediately.

"Mr. Prescott is in the powder room," I explained. "Should I wait for him here?"

"Follow me." He showed me to a small, hidden sitting area behind the foyer—where I imagined service workers and non-special guests must have to wait to see the lady of the house. It was much less luxurious than the rest of the ornately decorated rooms. David was about to walk away when I added, "It must be a lot of work to run a house as large as this."

He turned and smiled, though I could tell from the dimness in his eyes that he had no interest in talking with me. "Yes, it certainly keeps me on my toes." He tried to turn again.

I raised my voice and said quickly, "And Mrs. Wong must be a hard person to please."

"Ah, at times, though the lady of the house has always treated me and the rest of the staff well." He paused, assessing me. "Can I ask your reason for being here today?"

Ah, the drama had pulled him in, just as Dean said it would. I lowered my voice and motioned him forward. "I'm a private detective, actually." I pulled out my detective license and showed it to him.

His eyebrows rose. "Really?" I could see the machinations turning inside his brain. "Nothing wrong, I hope?"

I crossed my arms. "No, no, not with Mrs. Wong. She might have been witness to something, that's all."

He let out a held breath. "Oh, that's good."

The pause that came after was long. What else was I supposed to say? *Damn*, where was Dean? And what the hell was he doing that was taking so long?

He pivoted to walk away. "Well, if that's all..."

I smiled. "Of course, you must have a lot to do, don't let me keep you." As soon as he'd turned the corner I stood up and went around to watch the stairs. The housekeeper was gone. Had he gone up the stairs? Where was Dean? And why did I care so damn much? If he got caught that was all on him. This was *his* world, not mine.

"Miss me?" a voice from behind my ear called.

"*Shit.*" I whipped around to find Dean standing behind me. "How the hell did you get over there?" My heart pounded loudly in my chest. I tried to relax my face, but Dean smirked. He knew he'd gotten to me.

"I took the back stairs. This house is old. It still has a staircase for the servants so guests don't see them running around."

"Lovely." I schooled my expression and narrowed my eyes. "*Don't do that again.* What the hell were you looking for anyways?"

He motioned me forward and we left out the front door. The afternoon sun was warm as we neared golden hour.

"I was originally going to look through her personal bathroom and see if I could find that cologne—maybe it was her husbands or something, but then you'll never guess what I found in her desk instead."

"You went through her bedroom?" I was flabbergasted. "Don't you realize that's a crime?"

He shrugged casually. "We were invited in."

I gaped. Was he truly that ignorant? "That's not how that works and you know it."

He frowned, furrowing his brow. "Do you want to know what I found out or not?"

We got to the bottom of the steps and walked over to the car. I slid in the passenger side. "Fine, only I'm going to pretend whatever you saw, you saw it in the study, and that you didn't go snooping where you didn't belong."

He rolled his eyes. "Don't tell me you've never snooped, detective. Isn't that in your job description?"

"Not when it involves going places you're not legally allowed to be, no."

He pulled out his phone, unlocked it, and then handed it to me. "Take a look at that."

I scrolled through his most recent photos. There were stacks of documents sitting on a desk.

"Zoom in," he directed.

I looked over at him and frowned, but did as he said, focusing in on the papers. The one on top was a bill. A very overdue, very large bill, guessing by the number of zeros at the bottom.

Dean glanced my way before starting the car. "Our heiress is broke, apparently."

I swiped through the other photos—more documents—and went one slide too far. It was a photo of Dean and Felicity from last night's party, posing and laughing at the same time. I cleared my throat and handed his phone back to him. "I see what you mean. She has motive. I thought you said that she never left the lounge, though? And she *does* strike me as an odd choice for murder."

He shrugged. "She could be working with someone. I mean, she would have to be, right? It wasn't her that knocked you to the ground this morning?"

I shook my head. "Definitely not. Whoever knocked me over had strength and a weight to them. Cassidy Wong is barely five foot and in her sixties."

"Exactly. So if she was involved, she would have hired someone or made a deal with them."

I jotted down the idea and put my notepad back in my jacket pocket. "Let's not get too ahead of ourselves here. We still have a lot of people to talk to, and Mrs. Wong just told us Tyler Conrad has sticky fingers. He might be exactly who we're looking for."

Dean revved the engine as we passed through the security gate. "If you say so. I'm simply suggesting that we don't underestimate people."

I smiled. "Trust me, Dean, I never underestimate anyone."

He caught my eye. "I'll keep that in mind, detective."

EIGHT

We pulled up to a red light, the setting sun painting gold across the hills. "I'll get the address from Lexi. It shouldn't be too hard to find out where Conrad lives."

Dean grinned. "It's probably on some celebrity watch list online."

I pulled out my phone to text Lexi, only a song started playing in the car—loud trumpets and piano, an old-school Bond theme song.

Dean cringed and pulled out his own phone to answer it. "That's me."

Now it was making more sense why he'd wanted to accompany me on the interviews. He was probably obsessed with thrillers and detective stories. It was always rich people who found themselves bored as a log doing the craziest things. Thrill seekers. I knew there was something up with him. I rolled my eyes out of view as he put the phone to his ear.

"Hello?" His smile faded at whatever the person on the other side of the line said. "Okay, I can be there in fifteen minutes. Yes." He hung up and dropped his phone in the center console.

"Be *where* in fifteen minutes?" I asked, crossing my arms over my chest.

He turned to catch my gaze. "That was Detective Warner. He wants to interview me again down at the station."

"Already? They just took your statement a few hours ago." I scoffed. "I bet they lost the transcript," I said under my breath.

"That doesn't make me feel better."

I turned to look back at Dean. He wasn't smiling anymore. His face was filled with what I could only describe as pure nerves, his lips pressed together, his brow furrowed. Just like when he was talking to the cops the first time.

I cleared my throat. "Sorry. It's really no big deal. He most likely wants to go over your statement again, probably because they haven't come up with any good leads yet. He'll most likely try to trip you up, because he's an ass. Just stay calm and call your lawyer if you feel you need to. They can't withhold your rights."

We stopped at another light and he turned to me. "Will you come with me?"

"I..." I really should interview Conrad before it got too late. This case was moving quickly and there was no reason to slow down now.

"Please? I would really appreciate you being there." His voice was so earnest and quiet, not like his usual brash, loud personality.

"I suppose I could be there. I'm not a lawyer, though. It's not a guarantee they'll let me in the room. Not if Warner has a say in it."

He let out a deep breath. "Okay, thank you, detective."

God, this guy had me all twisted up. I *should* hate him. He represented everything I despised about society—a rich party boy interviewing murder suspects for the thrill of it? Though at the same time, there was a vulnerability there that I wanted to protect. Nobody should have to be grilled by Warner over a murder they didn't commit, even rich, overbearing assholes. "Hey, you're the one paying me, this is all billable hours," I reminded him.

He gave me a wry smile. "I accept the charges."

I shrugged. "Besides, I'd like to see the look on Warner's face when you lawyer up. He doesn't like being told no. He'll get all red in the face and pissy."

Dean chuckled, catching my eye as he sped along the road.

* * *

Dean made a flurry of phone calls as he traced the route back to Hollywood and the police station. Most of it sounded like complete nonsense to me. When Dean ended the last phone call he explained, "My usual lawyer is out of town for a golf tournament, so they're sending one of the partners to cover for him."

"What terrible timing."

"What terrible golf skills," he said as he turned the corner from Sunset onto Wilcox. "He placed fourteenth out of fifteen in his last tournament. But he's determined to medal this time around."

The parking lot of the Hollywood Police Station was packed on a weekend night. We had to park on the street and pay the meter. "How long do you think they'll grill me?" Dean asked as he put quarters into the old-school parking meter.

"At least a few dollars," I replied as he dumped in the last of his coins. "They might try and make you sweat by leaving you in the room for a while."

He paled. "I thought they only did that in movies?"

"Nope, it's one of their best tactics, actually. You'd be surprised how many people spill information simply because they're bored out of their minds or racked with guilt and nerves."

We walked side by side to the front of the station. Inside was a sterile white lobby area with cheap metal folding chairs lining either wall. In front of us was a clear acrylic booth that surrounded the front desk. I recognized the officer sitting behind it.

"Detective Sun, back so soon?" he asked with the low, rumbly voice of a lifelong smoker.

"Only to see you, big guy."

He laughed and glanced at his computer screen. "Why are you here today?"

"My client, Mr. Prescott, is being interviewed by Warner. Has his representation arrived yet?"

He scrolled through a page. "Nope, just you two. I don't know if Warner is going to want you back there, though."

Dean leaned in. "He's my special counsel. I can have more than one, can't I?"

Officer Watts hummed and tapped his fingers on the desk. "It's not standard, but I'll let you both go in and we'll let Warner decide. Don't blame me if he kicks you out."

"Thanks Watts." I made a clicking sound with my mouth and pointed at him. "I owe you."

He chuckled. "I know, I'm keeping a list of 'em."

I waved my hand. "Yeah, yeah, don't get greedy."

He buzzed us in and we passed through to the back of the station. The office was one big open space with desks laid out in clusters. Most of them were empty with officers milling around in groups throughout the room.

A tall Black woman with a bob of bright red hair was sitting in a chair close to us as we passed. She smiled, her dark red lips parting. "Hi there, detective, it's been a while."

I waved. "Hey, Candy. Not staying out of trouble, I see?"

She shrugged and gave me a small wave, her wrists bound in handcuffs. "A girl's got to make a living somehow."

Watts led us into the back where we entered a small interview room —empty except for a plain plastic desk and two plastic folding chairs. "I'll let him know you're here."

I nodded at him. "Thanks."

Dean sat down in one chair and I leaned up against the nearest wall.

"So...Candy, huh?" Dean asked with a smirk.

I rolled my eyes and crossed my arms. "She hired me a year ago to find and arrest her ex-boyfriend."

He raised a brow. "And why would she do that?"

"Because he left her with a black eye and she wanted some peace of mind knowing where he was."

His expression fell. "Oh. Shit."

"Yeah, I get all kinds of clients." I shrugged. "Not always who you would expect."

"So I'm guessing I wasn't your first murder case?"

I shook my head. "No, I've worked a few. That's how I first met Warner and his old partner, Crawfield. He hasn't changed much since then, still an ass."

Dean grinned and tapped his fingers against the plastic table, his eyes drilling into the wall.

I'd been wanting to ask him something since this morning, only I didn't know if he'd want to talk about it. I figured in an interview room was as good a place as any. "When you found the body earlier, that wasn't your first time seeing a dead person, was it?" I asked slowly.

His smile faded. "Uh, no. How could you tell?"

I shrugged one shoulder. "Well, most people either do the screaming thing or they do the frozen and speechless thing. You seemed...okay, I guess."

He laughed through his nose. "I wouldn't say that I was *okay*, but I managed, I suppose."

"So, who was it?" Was that prying too much? We barely knew each other, after all.

"Which time?" he replied.

"Really?" I was surprised. I'd always thought of young, rich guys like him as untouchable. Problems seemed to bounce right off of them.

"Unfortunately, having a nice house and a nice car doesn't protect you from getting cancer," he replied, seeming to read my mind.

"I'm sorry." I shouldn't have brought it up. It was none of my business.

"It is what it is." He shifted in the chair, crossing his legs the other way. "My mom died when I was seven. My father insisted on having an open casket funeral even though she'd lost all her hair and she'd been whittled away from the chemo and the morphine. She didn't look like my mother at all, more like a ghost than a person." His eyes met mine. "My father started drinking pretty heavily after that. He lasted another ten years until I was about to graduate high school, then it caught up to him —liver failure. You can't get on the liver donation list unless you've been sober for at least six months and my father wasn't sober a day in his adult life."

Damn. He said it all so matter-of-factly, and yet I could tell it hurt more than he was letting on—his cramped body language, his eyes that darted between the plastic table and me.

"That's intense."

He looked up again and seemed to pull himself back together with a smile. "Is it? Sorry, I kinda got lost in memories for a second." He straightened his posture. "So yeah, death doesn't scare me, detective."

A door slammed down the hall and I was reminded of where we were—the police station, about to be interviewed for an ongoing murder investigation. Now was not the time to get sappy, especially with a client. We had a professional work relationship and it needed to stay that way. "Good to know."

We waited for another few minutes listening to the white noise of the office—phones ringing, people talking, and the quiet hum of the radio playing oldies in the background. The door to the interview room flew open and Warner strolled in, his eyes focused on the folder of papers in his hand.

"Mr. Prescott, your lawyer is here. Why you would need one, I don't know." Warner already sounded annoyed. *Good.*

Warner's partner Caruso walked in behind him and another man after that—an older White guy with salt and pepper hair and a chiseled jaw. He looked more like a model who'd walked out of a cologne ad than a lawyer.

Dean stood to shake his hand. "Thanks for coming, Martin."

"Of course, Mr. Prescott. Always here to help." He leaned in closer and dropped his voice. "Don't answer any questions without checking with me first, okay?"

I wondered how much his retainer was. Ten thousand a year? More?

Warner rolled his eyes. "Your client is not on trial, this is a simple interview to understand the nature of his involvement with the deceased."

"Which Mr. Prescott has already told you is none," I quipped.

Warner looked over as if just noticing I was there. "Mr. Sun, you didn't have any other place to be tonight? No dirty pictures to capture for some angry housewife?"

I laughed at the poor attempt at a dig. "I'm here to make sure my client's rights aren't being violated."

He smiled. "Isn't that what this one is for?" He pointed to the GQ Man of The Year.

"It never hurts to get a second opinion, does it?" Dean added.

Caruso, who was standing in the back, chuckled until Warner gave him the evil eye to shut him up. "Whatever, let's just get this started." He sat down in the chair on the other side of Dean and laid out the papers that were in the folder. "I need to confirm some things from your statement, Mr. Prescott."

He nodded. "Confirm away."

"You were hosting a party at your uncle's house last night from 10:30 until two in the morning?"

"Yes."

"And everyone you invited were people you didn't know personally?"

"Well yes, everyone except my friend Felicity.

"And the deceased was not one of your guests?"

He shook his head. "No."

Warner pulled out a glossy crime scene photo and placed it face up in front of Dean. "And you say that you've never seen this man before?"

He glanced down at the image, though I could tell he was trying not to. "Never in my life."

Warner went on, "I wanted to ask your uncle, Mr. Williams, if he knew the victim, only it seems that we're unable to get ahold of him through the number you provided to us." He read off the number from a sheet of paper in his file folder. "Is that the correct number?"

"Yes." Dean turned toward his lawyer who nodded. "My uncle is on a boat in the middle of the Greek islands. He probably won't have any cell service until he reaches his next destination."

"Which would be when?"

Dean shrugged. "I don't know. My uncle didn't exactly give me an itinerary of his trip before he left."

"Have you spoken to him since yesterday?"

"No, I haven't been able to reach him either, obviously." Dean looked away and crossed his arms.

Warner scoffed. "*Obviously?*"

"You have the same number I do. If you can't reach him, what makes you think *I* can?"

Warner leaned across the desk, no doubt trying to look intimidating. "And you have no other way of reaching him? No handlers or numbers to call?"

Dean shrugged. "You could try contacting the Greek coast guard or something. Does Greece have a coast guard?"

Warner *did not* look amused. "The statue that was stolen from Mr.William's house. How much did you say it was worth?"

Dean waved his hand. "Four million, give or take."

"And have you been having any sort of financial issues, Mr. Prescott?"

Dean narrowed his eyes, his lips pressed together into a tight line. "What are you implying?" His lawyer started to say something, and Dean held up his hand. "That I stole the statue myself? Why would I do that? I don't need the money."

"And would you be willing to let us look at your accounts to prove that?" Warner asked.

"No, because I don't need to prove myself and you have no right to look at my finances. Is this what you're focusing on instead of looking for the killer?"

Warner smiled, his expression tight. "We're looking at all possibilities, Mr. Prescott. Everything is on the table."

"I'm sure. Do you know *anything* about the victim?"

"We know he was stabbed with a small-bladed knife—probably a pocket knife—eleven times in the chest. Do you own a pocket knife, Mr. Prescott?"

Dean rolled his eyes, blatantly now. "No, detective, I don't. I was never a Boy Scout." He tapped his fingers on the table. "Is that all you have?"

Warner looked up from Dean to catch my eye and then glanced back down. "That's all that you need to know at this time, Mr. Prescott."

Asshole. He was withholding any new information they had. Hopefully he was bluffing.

Warner sighed and leaned back in his chair. "One more question, Mr. Prescott. Did you touch the body or anything around the body before the police arrived?"

Oh shit, I was afraid he was going to ask that.

"No, of course not." He lied so effortlessly he almost had *me* convinced it was the truth. "Mr. Sun made sure we kept the crime scene clean." He looked over his shoulder at me and winked.

Damn him.

The lawyer piped up, "Are we done here? My client has places to be."

Warner gritted his teeth, his jaw clenching. "I'm sure he does. Fine. Just don't think about leaving the city. We'll need to talk to you again if we can't contact your uncle."

"Don't worry, detective, I'm not going anywhere." Dean smiled and stood, straightening his suit jacket and brushing off his trousers.

Once we made our way outside, Dean shook hands with his lawyer, and the man left in a bright red convertible. He'd said all of ten words and he'd made thousands of dollars in twenty minutes. Nice gig.

"That went about as well as I'd expected," Dean said as we reached his car.

"Did it?"

He turned, his smile dropping a fraction. "Thanks for being there, I know you could probably think of better ways to move this investigation forward."

I shook my head. "Seeing Warner squirm was worth it. I was glad to be there."

"So what now?" He glanced down at his watch. "Are we interviewing Tyler Conrad?"

I glanced at my phone. "*Hmm*, something tells me that we're not going to be able to see him tonight."

"Why's that?"

I showed him the text that Lexi had sent me. It was a social media post about the rager that Conrad was throwing at his mansion. "I don't think that's going to be over for a while."

He grinned. "Isn't that a good thing? Interviewing people while they're drunk?"

I chuckled. "In my experience, no actually. Alcohol is not the truth serum people think it is. We're more likely to get no information and puke on our shoes than a lead. Better to interview him in the morning when he's hung over. People will say anything to get someone to shut up when they have a headache."

He grinned and snapped his fingers at me. "Good thinking."

We got in the car and Dean dropped me off on the east side in front of the office. "What time should I pick you up?" he asked.

"I do own a car, Dean. You don't have to drive me around like some kind of passenger prince."

He smirked. "Why, does it bother you?"

I got out of the car and put my hands in my jacket pockets. "No, I just like driving myself."

"So you like being in control?" I didn't say anything as he revved the engine. "I'll pick you up at eight. Get some rest, detective."

As he peeled away into the night I pulled out my phone and made a note to add up my billable hours for the day. Dean might have been annoying, however he was also my best paying client of the month, maybe the year.

I walked up the stairs to the office and found it empty. Lexi had left a note at the front desk.

Dad called, so I went home. I'll send you what else I can dig up on Tyler Conrad in the morning.

That kid worked too hard. I reminded myself to track *her* billable hours as well. I made sure that every cent I paid her—when I could—got put into her college fund. My brother Mark, her dad, wasn't too happy about taking money from me, the proud bastard. But I'd convinced him that it was *Lexi* who had earned the money, so it was really *her* money, not *mine*. Which was true. Though, sometimes I paid her even when things were tight, and took a pay cut for myself, while paying her her full share.

I locked up the front door and the office before marching upstairs to the apartment. Captain greeted me at the door with slobbery tongue kisses to my hands and arms. "Hey, boy. Sorry you got neglected all day. What do you say we go on a walk?" Those were the magic words. He jumped up on me, panting.

I was halfway down the street before I realized I hadn't eaten all day, neither had Dean. We'd been so in the thick of the investigation I'd forgotten. I did that sometimes. It made me miss Malcolm. He'd been nagging and we'd argued a lot, but he would always remind me to eat, even if it was only instant ramen eaten hastily sitting on my kitchen floor.

Ramen.

Seeing as how I was going to be flush in a few days from Dean's deposit I splurged on *real* ramen—a place around the corner from my apartment that didn't mind if Captain sat on the floor under the table. I savored the warm, umami broth and my mind drifted to the case, the theft, the murder, Dean.

Maybe I should have invited him to eat ramen with me? Or would that have been strange? I shook away the thought. Dean wasn't a friend, he was a client. I needed to stay professional and get the job done. There wasn't time to mess around.

I checked my messages and found nothing. I'd contacted a couple art fences that I knew to see if they'd heard anything about the statue. Nobody had any information. Which either meant the statue was already long gone, or it was being sold under more unusual channels. A deal this big was bound to make some noise. So where was it?

I slurped up a noodle. This case was turning out to be way more complicated than I'd anticipated. Tomorrow was going to be an extremely long day.

NINE

"Morning, detective." Dean grinned from the driver's seat. He was dressed in a soft gray striped suit with a gold tie that brought out his brown eyes. His dark hair was styled meticulously, no doubt with expensive creams and potions us common folk couldn't dream of affording.

"Good morning." I'd already gone for a run with Captain and had a briefing with Lexi on the phone. She was working from home today since her parents thought she'd spent too long at the office yesterday. Did it violate child labor laws if she was my niece?

"Coffee?" Dean held out a paper cup he'd plucked from the center console.

"Oh, thank you." Clients didn't usually bring me coffee, so it was a nice surprise. I took the cup as I slid into the passenger seat. I wasn't missing my Jeep so much this morning, what with fancy convertibles and coffee in hand.

"I didn't know how you liked it, so I settled for black," he explained.

I nodded. "That's how I like it."

His lips tugged into a warm smile. "Good." He turned over the engine. "So, any word from your art contacts about the statue?"

I shook my head. "Nobody has heard anything, which is either good or terrible."

Dean sucked on his teeth. "I'm going to hope for the first option. Maybe whoever stole it hasn't placed it on the market yet? They're waiting for things to cool off?"

I nodded. "That's what I'm hoping too. So I think our time is better spent working at it from a different angle, tracing the statue back from the thief."

Dean revved the engine and pulled around a bend. "Okay. So what's the story? Are we storming the castle, or what?"

I gestured with my hand for him to slow down. "Not storming, *gently entering*."

He faced me with a smirk. "And who's the good cop?"

"What?"

"You know, good cop, bad cop? Who's gonna play the nice guy and who's gonna be the jerk? Are you the asshole?"

I scowled.

He laughed. "See? You got the look down already."

I rolled my eyes and said firmly, "Nobody is *playing* anything. *I'm* the detective, remember, Dean?"

He frowned, his plush lips pouting. "You're no fun, Dad."

"Dad? You're maybe two years younger than me, who the hell are you calling Dad?"

He chuckled. "It was just an expression, detective. Calm down. We'll play it by ear then, huh?" He turned the car around the corner into the hills.

"I'll ask the questions, you can stand there and look pretty. Like we did yesterday."

"So you think I'm pretty?" Dean asked before laughing.

Warmth crept up my neck and I pinched the bridge of my nose. "I need some more coffee before I can handle this." I took a swig of the black elixir and stayed silent for the rest of the drive. I didn't think it was possible for Dean to have even more boyish energy than before, but apparently yesterday he'd been toned down from all the trauma.

"So what do we know about our golden boy?" Dean asked as we passed the first security gate.

"Um." I pulled up Lex's notes on the topic. "Tyler Conrad: twenty-six, heir to the Conrad real estate dynasty and partial owner of more than five film studios out of Burbank. He's been kicked out of three private schools and two universities for lewd behavior and fighting. He throws a lot of parties and funds many social media influencer's ventures. From what Mrs. Wong has told us he has sticky fingers and no boundaries."

"So what's his motive if he doesn't need the money?"

I shrugged. "The thrill? He wanted to up his game?"

Dean laughed through his nose. "That's a large leap from pickpocketing to stealing a four million dollar antiquity."

"Stranger things have happened."

Dean turned his head. "Does he have the skills?"

"We'll find out. One of the schools he dropped out of was MIT, so obviously he has *some* intelligence, unless his parents bought his way in. He's a good suspect, we'll have to see what he says."

We pulled up to Conrad's gated estate up in the Hollywood Hills. "Does he know we're coming?" I asked.

Dean grinned. "I made an appointment in advance this time." He said something into the security system's intercom and the white wrought iron gate swung open.

"How did you convince him to see us?"

"You get more flies with honey than vinegar, detective. I simply asked nicely."

I scoffed. "And that worked?"

He shrugged. "Drink up, it's go time."

I downed what was left of my coffee as Dean pulled into the long circular drive. There was evidence of last night's party strewn on the lawn that a gardener in coveralls was currently cleaning up—champagne flutes, party streamers, masks. What kind of party had this been?

We rang the front door and the housekeeper showed us to the backyard where there was an olympic-sized swimming pool and a luxurious cabana. It appeared like the backyard had already been cleaned with no trace of the party we'd seen out front. "Mr. Conrad?" the housekeeper said. "Two gentlemen are here to see you, a Mr. Prescott and a Mr. Sun."

Tyler Conrad was laying out on a beach chair wearing only a pair of short blue swim trunks. He had his eyes closed and his arms facing up, glistening with suntan lotion. "What can I do for you, gentlemen?" he said, not seeming to think it was strange we were there at all.

"Are we disturbing you?" I asked, annoyed at his casual position.

He raised his brows. "Not at all. I'm just getting my daily dose of vitamin D. It does wonders for the immune system."

"I'm sure. We want to talk to you about the party Friday night at Mr. Prescott's place," I said, getting straight to the point.

Conrad opened one eye. "Oh?"

Dean smiled. "Yes. You *do* remember being there, don't you?"

I gave Dean the evil eye and he frowned. He couldn't help himself, could he?

Conrad nodded. "Uh, sure, I remember the party. It was at that old house, right? With the library?"

Dean caught my eye. "The library? The party was in the lounge."

Conrad waved his hand. "Same difference."

I could tell where Dean's question was leading. The library was in the part of the house that was out of bounds to guests, or it was *supposed* to be. So Conrad *had* been wandering around like Miguel and Mrs. Wong had informed us.

Clearly he wasn't easily intimidated. I leaned down over him. "Something was taken from the house during that party, Mr. Conrad. Something very valuable."

He opened both eyes; finding me so close made him smile. "Valuable? It was only a stupid pen, how valuable could it be?"

Okay, *now* I was confused.

"A pen?" Dean asked, equally as surprised.

Conrad frowned. "Isn't that what we're talking about here? The pen I took from the library?"

I crossed my arms and took a step back. "Uh, well no, actually."

"Oh." He pulled a lever and sat up in the chair, apparently done with his tanning. "I assumed that's what you came here for. Are you saying something else was taken?"

"Yes," Dean replied.

He shrugged. "I don't know anything about that. I only took the pen. I can give it back to you if you wait a moment."

Before I could get a word in he'd already gotten up, ran off down the walkway, and slipped inside the house.

"What the hell?" Dean said, which encapsulated everything I was thinking.

Conrad came back a few minutes later, a gauzy white robe wrapped around his near-naked body. "Here, sorry about that. I have a bad habit of taking things. I never could understand why." He held out an expensive-looking fountain pen that was probably a dime a dozen to someone like Dean or his uncle.

"Uh, thank you?" Dean said, accepting the stolen item.

"I hope we don't have to take things further because then I'd have to get my father involved and it becomes a whole mess," he said as if it was a standard Sunday morning to have a private detective banging at your door.

"Well, no, I don't really care about the pen," Dean said. "I care about the statue that was stolen from the study the same night."

Conrad's eyebrows shot up. "Oh, shit. Really? That sucks." He seemed genuinely sympathetic, which was even more puzzling.

"You didn't see anyone wandering around when you were...taking that pen, did you?" I asked.

Conrad cocked his head to the side in thought. "Hmm, I mean I saw a couple people, I think. I saw Miguel once, I saw that influencer girl, and I saw that burly guy as well—the one with all the crazy tattoos. Oh, plus the catering staff. You don't think it was one of them, do you?" he asked, intrigue in his eyes.

"We don't think so, but thanks." I wrote down the descriptions in my notepad. "Anything else you can remember from that night that stood out?"

He mused for a second. "The canapés were good. Usually they're pretty shit at those kinds of parties, but those squid things were excellent."

Dean grinned, his eyes expressing that he was over this conversation. "I'll give your compliments to the chef."

I couldn't tell if Tyler Conrad was an idiot or confident as hell. Maybe both.

"And where were you yesterday morning between eight and nine?"

He squinted against the sun. "Why do you want to know?"

"There was a second break-in that morning."

His eyebrows rose. "Wow, you are very unlucky."

Dean smiled and crossed his arms. "Thanks."

"So?" I prompted.

"As long as we're being truthful here, I was sleeping with my tennis partner. She can confirm that for me, only don't go to her house. She's married, and that would really piss her off."

"Good to know. Thanks for answering our questions," I said. "If we have any more we'll contact you."

Tyler grinned. "No problem. My housekeeper has something for you to sign before you leave."

"Something to sign?" I asked slowly, already annoyed again.

Dean leaned in and whispered, "NDA's, probably."

"Just a precaution, you understand," Tyler explained in a smooth, casual tone.

No, I *didn't* understand. Maybe he *was* more calculated than I'd previously thought.

"Have a nice day, guys. It's gonna be a sunny one." He disrobed and dove into the pool with an impressive arc, dismissing us.

Dean laughed at my expression as we were led through the house to the front door. The housekeeper had a paper for each of us to sign. Dean was right, they were non-disclosure agreements. Basically if we said anything about Tyler's habit of stealing from strangers we'd be sued for damages. *Fun.* I handed back my signed copy with a grimace. I hated being forced to do things I didn't agree with.

As we slipped out the front door Dean slapped my arm with the back of his hand. "Cheer up, detective, there are worse things."

"Oh I know, and they're probably happening on this very street." I gestured to the rest of the upper-class neighborhood.

"Probably." Dean walked ahead of me. "So, he stole a pen, do we think he stole anything else?"

I slipped into the passenger seat as Dean hopped in the front. "I don't think he's our guy. He could be working with someone like you suggested, although it's not likely. I think MIT was a fluke, he seems like more of the hot and dumb type."

Dean raised a brow. "So maybe someone with brains is controlling him?"

"*Hmm*, maybe. I suppose Mrs. Wong could be blackmailing him into working for her, but then why tell us about his stealing? Is it a double bluff? And then why was he so forthcoming about who he saw in the hallway?"

"He could *still* be working with someone else. Maybe he only gave us those descriptions to throw us off his partner, to distract us," Dean suggested.

I chewed on the idea. "Possibly. He *is* the right height and weight for whoever ran me down yesterday, that's one strike against him if his alibi turns out to be bullshit."

"So was Miguel," Dean added.

"God, we need more evidence, these interviews aren't helping much. We need something more concrete. I was hoping somebody would contradict each other, however everyone has been on the same page so far."

Dean turned down the sloping hill. "I might know a guy who could look at the security equipment. That could tell us something, right?"

"Your house is still a crime scene," I reminded him.

"My guy could be in and out. Discreet."

I turned to catch his eye. "You sure seem to know a lot of people who do a lot of things...discreetly."

He smiled. "That's Hollywood, baby. All my friends have their fingers in the pie."

"So what do *you* bring to the table?" I asked without thinking.

He laughed. "I'm the financier, detective. The money man."

I leaned my arm against the back of the seat. "That must get old, friends asking you for money."

He shrugged. "It's a delicate line, although I'm more than happy to help someone out if I see potential."

We stopped at a red light on the edge of the Beverly Hills strip. Tourists were walking down Rodeo in droves.

"Where to next?" Dean asked.

I read through the list Lexi had texted me. "Everly Sanderson, beauty influencer. She was at your party looking for investors for her new makeup line, Raw-Love Beauty. Do you remember her?"

Dean nodded. "Yes, I'm the one that invited her. We met at a party last week. She seemed like a nice enough girl. Can't say I know anything about her."

"So, according to Lexi: she's twenty-eight, she comes from a rich family, and she doesn't appear to have any money troubles."

"Other than needing investors."

"Yes, other than that. But would someone really resort to stealing an antiquity to fund a makeup line? Besides, you'd never met her before, right? So she couldn't have known the statue was going to be there, which would make it a crime of opportunity. It doesn't fit. This was definitely planned. How else could someone have gotten past your security?"

"I guess that's true," Dean conceded. "Unless she's working with someone else?"

"Which seems to be what we keep coming back to. Let's just talk to her and see what she has to say." I gave him the address and we crossed town into West Hollywood where her makeup studio was.

The studio was a small, hole-in-the-wall space; we almost missed it. There were no signs or branding, only a suite number. The glass door was covered in white paint from the inside so nobody could look in. Mysterious already. Dean knocked on the door. Then we waited, and waited, and waited.

"Maybe nobody's home?" Dean suggested.

"*Maybe.*" I was curious what a rich girl like Everly would be doing renting a crappy studio like this on the edge of West Hollywood? One that was apparently boarded up for business.

He knocked one more time.

"Hello?" a voice called from down the street. A tall woman with chestnut hair and a svelte figure walked toward us. She certainly *looked* like a beauty influencer, every inch of her face was painted, down to her cherry-red lipstick. She was covered in jewels to match—necklace, earrings, and bracelets.

"Everly Sanderson?" I asked.

She nodded and then noticed Dean behind me. "Oh, Dean." She smiled. "What are you doing here? Did you change your mind about my makeup line?"

Dean gave her a lopsided grin. "Not exactly, we had a couple of questions for you. Can we step inside?"

She laughed and rolled her eyes. "Oh, actually, there's nowhere *to* step inside. Not yet, anyway." She gestured to the studio. "It's a construction zone in there, a total mess; we're getting ready for the new retail flagship space."

Ah, that explained why the windows were covered up.

"There's a café around the corner," she pointed behind her, "if you want to sit down and talk?"

Dean shrugged. "Sure, why not."

We followed her to the café where Dean ordered a sandwich and another coffee, Everly ordered a matcha, and I ordered nothing. I didn't like to eat while interviewing someone, it was too casual. We weren't friends. Dean didn't seem to have that problem. He took a bite of his sandwich and asked, "So how's the makeup line going? I'm sorry I couldn't invest this quarter."

Her cherry lips pulled apart revealing bright white teeth. "That's okay, it was still nice to be invited to your event. Being in that room filled with powerful people felt correct for me."

Cocky.

"We really wanted to talk to you because of something that happened during the party." I explained that an object of great value was stolen and that a bunch of people had been wandering around in the back halls, including herself.

She pinched her brows together. "Oh no, that's terrible. I'm sorry, Dean."

He shrugged and smiled politely. "Thanks."

"So did you see anything while you were in the back of the house?" I asked, eager to get this show on the road. We didn't have time to waste eating sandwiches and drinking tea.

She pressed her lips together. "*Hmm*, I remember seeing the big blonde guy, Tyler. I saw Miguel—though he was on his phone, so I don't think he saw me—and uh, a little incident happened."

"An *incident*?" I asked.

She blushed. "I was looking for the bathroom—you know how all the doors in that house look the same with the wooden paneling—when

I accidentally opened a closet instead and found the two servers in uh...a compromising position."

"Wow." Dean grinned ear-to-ear, like the child that he was.

"I was so embarrassed, I hurried back to the lounge and I stayed there the rest of the party."

"Do you remember what time that was?"

She nodded. "I'll never forget, it was just after midnight—the grandfather clock in the hallway was chiming, that's how I remember."

I guess that more or less confirmed the server's alibis, and the statements from Tyler and Miguel.

"Did you see anything else unusual?" Dean asked.

She mused, placing her chin in her hand. "Not really, unless you count that tattooed guy. I thought he was sort of a strange guest. Did you know him, Dean?"

Dean shook his head. "Not a clue. I think Felicity invited him. He *was* a bit odd, wasn't he?"

Two strikes for the big tattooed guy. We'd need to check on him soon.

"And one last question. Can I ask what you were doing yesterday morning between eight and nine?"

She pinched her brows. "Um, okay. I think I was at the nail salon, if I'm remembering right." She glanced down at her phone and scrolled through something, probably her calendar. "Yep, 8:15. Why do you want to know?"

I shrugged. "We're asking everyone. There was a disturbance at the house during that time."

She looked between us. "*Another* disturbance?"

Dean sighed. "Yes, I've had rather rotten luck this week."

"Yeah." I smiled politely. "Well, thank you for answering our questions. If we have any more we'll be sure to contact you."

She smiled and patted Dean's hand on the table. "Anything I can do to help. I'm sorry this happened to you."

Dean shrugged, like it was nothing.

We parted ways and went back to the car, leaving Everly in the café. "Well? What do you think?" Dean asked.

I hummed. "I don't know. She seemed pretty genuine."

"I agree."

"And what motive does she have?" I went on. "She doesn't really need the money like some of our other suspects and she stayed in the lounge for most of the night. The only time she left she was seen by at least four people." I got in the car and turned to face Dean. "I think we need your guy."

He grinned wildly, as if he'd been waiting for me to tell him that. "You got it." He pulled out his phone and started typing. After a minute or two he said, "He's going to meet us at the house. He says he should have no problem checking when the system was deactivated as long as it's still functioning. Are the cops going to be an issue?"

I shrugged, raising my brows. "I guess we'll find out when we get there."

TEN

When we pulled up to the house the driveway was empty—no cops, no keep out signs. The place was suspiciously abandoned. "Huh, either they gave up already, or they're very confident who they think killed that guy."

"Why?" Dean parked the car right in front of the stairs.

I gestured at the house. "Because they don't usually clean up this fast. Someone was killed here yesterday."

He shrugged. "I might have told my lawyer to pressure them into finishing early."

I balked. "What?" Rich people operated by a totally different set of rules; it made my head spin.

"I've played golf with the police commissioner's son once or twice. That might have helped."

"You think?" I got out of the car and walked up the steps. Caution tape was still covering the front door in an X. "Let's hope they didn't miss anything," I mumbled. I was all for getting Warner and his lapdog out of the way, but the people on the forensics team were the real unsung heroes. No reason to kick them out early.

"I don't think they had much to find. Whoever killed that guy was careful to cover their tracks. The only real evidence they have is the body, and *apparently* they can't get anything from that, either."

"Yeah." I at least agreed on *that* point.

Dean unlocked the door and pushed it open. The foyer where the body had been was completely cleared, blood and all.

"You're going to have to hire someone to clean that floor professionally." I pointed to the faint stain on the black and white marble.

He pulled his brows together. "Nah, we can clean it up in no time."

"*We?*" I wasn't being paid to clean some rich guy's house. I was a *private detective.*

He smiled. "Sorry, slip of the tongue. *I'll* clean it up in no time."

"That's better." I took a couple steps forward and looked around. "So when's your guy getting here?"

"I'm here."

The deep voice behind me made me jump. I spun around. *"Jesus."*

"No, the name's Charlie, actually." He was a short, square man with a dark beard, standing with his hands in his hoodie pocket.

I frowned and stepped aside for Dean to shake his hand.

Dean smiled. "Thanks for coming on such short notice, Charlie, I'm in a bit of a pickle."

Charlie looked between me and Dean. "I can see that."

What was that supposed to mean?

"So you can get into the security system?" I asked, to focus the topic of discussion to the task at hand.

He shrugged, his whole demeanor casual. "Sure, as long as it's Matlock, Verotech or SwiftCrypt, you're golden." He closed the front door. "Where's the control panel?"

Dean pointed behind us. "It's on the wall by the office."

I hadn't seen it the last time we'd walked through the house. I'd been too busy running after Dean's yelling and then dealing with a dead body.

We walked across the house to the back halls of the west wing and Charlie started to examine the panel. It was small and white with a square, lit-up screen. It was so flat it almost blended into the wooden paneling of the wall.

Charlie pulled a slim bag from his shoulder and grabbed a few different colored cords from it. He plugged one into the control panel and the other into his tablet.

"So, do you work for a security company?" I asked, confused how Dean knew this guy.

After a pause he said, "Not exactly."

"And this is...legal?" I raised an eyebrow. I didn't want to make this already murky case any dirtier with dubious *friends* of Dean's.

Dean grinned. "It's my uncle's house that I've been entrusted with. Can't I hire whomever I want, to do whatever I want?"

I crossed my arms and narrowed my eyes. "*Hmm*, no, I don't think that's how that works." Actually, I was *sure* it wasn't.

"Lighten up, sourpuss." Dean clapped my back. "You said you wanted more evidence."

"Well I didn't think we'd have to put one past the cops and your uncle to do it."

Dean frowned, but said nothing as Charlie worked. I didn't understand half of what he was doing. His tablet was lit up with data, though most of it seemed like complete nonsense to me.

After a few quiet minutes Charlie smiled. "Very tricky."

"What?" Dean asked, hovering over Charlie's shoulder to look at the screen.

"Whoever had access to this system uploaded their own code."

Dean furrowed his brow. "Meaning?"

He went on, "They programmed the system to disarm itself without turning off the lights and sounds it usually makes."

I leaned in. "So it appeared like it was armed when it really wasn't?"

"Exactly. That takes some expert skill."

"Someone like you?" I asked.

He nodded. "At least."

I pointed at the stream of data. "So can you tell when this person did this?"

"Yeah, the code is timestamped." He clicked on something and pulled up a different box of raw code. "It looks like they added the program on Thursday night."

Dean's jaw dropped. "The night *before* the party, you mean?"

"Looks like."

"So this was definitely *not* a crime of passion, then." I turned to Dean. "When did you invite your guests?"

Dean shook his head in disbelief. "Different days. Some were invited a week before, some only the day of."

"Okay, we'll go over it later." I turned back to the screen. "Can you see when the sensor on the statue went off? Is that showing?"

He scrolled through his tablet and clicked on something. "Yes, since the statue was on a separate line from the rest of the house whoever manipulated the system wasn't able to disarm it completely. They changed it so that the system wouldn't automatically call the police, it redirected to call the owner of the house instead."

I almost laughed, catching Dean's eye. "So, your uncle? The unreachable one?"

He scowled. "*Damn.* What time?"

Charlie scrolled to the bottom. "The call was made at 12:13."

That was earlier than I'd thought in our time frame of midnight to two. "Does that take anyone off our suspect list?" I asked Dean. "Did anyone leave before midnight?"

He put his hands on his hips. "*Hmm*, I don't think so, but we can ask Felicity. She'd know for certain."

"How *is* Felicity?" Charlie asked. "It's been ages seen we've seen each other. She still kicking ass and taking names?"

Dean grinned. "Oh, you know it."

They said their goodbyes and Dean walked him out of the house. Charlie had fixed the security system, so hopefully there would be no more break-ins, and he'd also agreed to keep an eye on the house while we were investigating now that the cops were gone.

When Dean came back his face was neutral. "I really thought that was going to be more helpful."

"It *was* helpful," I argued. "We at least know for certain that this was planned and that you were being targeted."

He shrugged. "It doesn't help us sort out the timing of everything, though. Everly said that she was in the hallway right after midnight, that's when everyone else said that they were there as well. The statue was stolen at 12:13. So it could literally be any of them."

"It's too bad your uncle's house doesn't have cameras inside. That would have been informative."

His lips slowly pulled into a wide smile. "You're a genius!" He pulled me in for a tight hug, which caught me off guard.

"*What?*"

He beamed, pulling back and grabbing my shoulders. "My uncle is paranoid as shit, there probably *are* some secret cameras in this office. We just have to find them."

"Uh, okay." I followed him into the office and watched as he began to rummage around.

"It would probably be up high," I suggested, after catching Dean looking through the desk.

"You're right." He checked the corners of the room, feeling the plastered walls with his hand.

I decided to help out even though I thought his idea was silly. Why would his uncle entrust his security system to Dean and not mention the cameras? Then again, rich people were strange folk and did precisely what they wanted and *only* what they wanted. Maybe Dean was right.

I searched the bookshelf next to the entrance; it only contained real volumes—no secret book-cameras or fake tomes. The longer we searched the more discouraged I became. This was such a long shot. We should be interviewing our suspects again and creating a better timeline now that we knew when the statue was stolen definitively. Not that I was confident we would ever get the statue back. If someone was willing to kill for it the statue was probably long gone, in Saudi Arabia or some Italian villa on a new powerful millionaire's mantel.

"I don't think there's anything here," I said after maybe twenty minutes of looking.

Dean frowned, but nodded with defeat. "I guess you're probably right. Maybe my uncle is less paranoid than I thought."

We rearranged the desk back to its original condition and slipped out into the hallway.

"That was a waste of our time."

I agreed, only I didn't want him to feel bad about it. He'd been so excited over the prospect. "That's all part of the process. Finding the dead ends."

He glanced down the hall. "Guess I better go find something to clean up the mess in the lounge."

As Dean went to pass me I studied the molding above the door to the office. "Wait."

He stopped. "What?"

Something about the molding was off. It was different from the rest of the doors in the house. It wasn't something you would notice unless you were really looking for it. The lines were slightly off and the color was a shade too dark. "There." I pointed up as I raised my hand to pry at the piece. It came off with merely a touch. Clearly it wasn't made as part of the door's original frame.

"Oh shit."

Behind the fake molding was a small black dot of a camera connected to a wireless prong. "You were right, only he wasn't watching *inside* the office, he was watching *outside* the office."

Dean smacked his forehead. "God, I'm dumb. That makes way more sense, right?"

I pulled the camera off the wall with a gentle tug.

"So how do we see what was on it?" Dean asked.

I examined it more closely. "It looks wireless. I don't think it was made to store files. The videos are probably on your uncle's computer. Can you access it?" I asked.

Dean pinched his brows. "Uh...maybe?"

We went back into the office and after a fifteen minute phone call with Charlie—that I pretended I wasn't hearing—we got into the computer. The files weren't even concealed, just sitting on the main desktop labeled *West Hallway Hidden Camera*. Dean's uncle wasn't a subtle man, apparently.

Dean clicked on the folder and a series of files came up, all dated.

"There's Friday." I pointed to the icon and Dean clicked on the file. A video player popped up, twenty-four hours of footage. "Can you fast forward?"

He clicked through until the time was closer to the party. "There's me." He pointed at the screen as him and Felicity walked past around nine. "That's when I checked the perimeter. Then the caterers arrived right after. *Damn*, this video quality sucks."

"Agreed." The video was grainy, pixelated, and at an awkward angle, shooting down from above the door.

It took a minute to get to midnight, then he played the video at normal speed. "There's the two servers." Dean pointed out as they walked past the camera. Then came Max, then Everly, a few minutes later Miguel, then the big hulking guy with the tattoos, and then finally Conrad at 12:10. No one else walked past.

"There's only one way into that office, right?" I asked.

Dean nodded. "As far as I know. God, I hope I'm right."

"So we can confirm that Mrs. Wong didn't walk past until after the statue was stolen. Everyone else is fair game."

"No Mr. Hackney, either. I was talking with him for most of the night."

"So unless we had some partnerships going on we can take those two off our list of suspects for the theft."

"Right."

We were finally getting somewhere, finally able to start whittling down the pool of suspects. "So we know who we need to talk to next." I rewound the video until the big guy was walking past again. "Whoever this man is. Apparently, you don't even know."

Dean shrugged. "Felicity invited him. I can't keep track of everything and everyone at all times."

I started to copy the video file over to my phone, however the download was taking forever. After a few minutes Dean got impatient and walked out of the room. "What are you doing?" I asked.

He poked his head back in. "If he had one camera, maybe he had two? Maybe with a better, more helpful angle."

I shrugged. "I guess that's possible." I hadn't seen any files for a second camera, though that didn't mean it wasn't there.

The progress bar showed that the video was over halfway through being downloaded. It was a big file. "Check around the door frame, the paneling, and the picture frames. If they hid a second camera it would probably be hidden in a similar spot as the first," I suggested.

"Right."

I could hear Dean scuffling around, running his hand against the woodgrain. He didn't seem to be having much luck. The video was almost completely downloaded now.

WOOSH.

I tore my eyes from the screen and looked up. A metal door had dropped down across the entrance to the study. "Uh?" I got up and knocked on the door. "*Dean?*" A second later the door slowly retreated upwards into the molding of the doorframe. We hadn't noticed that either.

Dean was beaming on the other side of the doorway. "It looks like my uncle has some other fun toys as well."

"What was that?" I stepped out into the hall and Dean demonstrated. He slipped his hand underneath the nearest framed painting, gilded in gold. He pushed down on some small button and the metal door sliced through the air into place.

"It's a panic door," Dean said. "There must be a second button somewhere inside the office to lock yourself in," he pointed at the painting, "while this button locks your thieves out. Or maybe it's just another layer of precaution. Imagine having a heart attack while stuck in there with the only button that lets you in and out."

"Sounds like something out of a mystery book."

He grinned. "I knew my uncle was paranoid, but I'm learning so much today. I wonder if other rooms in the house have a panic door as well."

I shrugged. "At this rate, he probably has a whole secret bunker hidden around here somewhere."

"You know, you're probably not wrong. Although, my uncle is a vain man. He wouldn't hide his treasures away in a vault or something. He likes showing them off, displaying them."

"Hence the panic door and cameras."

Dean nodded. "Right."

I went back into the study to shut down the computer. Since Dean hadn't found a second camera (as far as we were aware) we'd have to work with the one video to further our investigation. As we were leaving the office my stomach rumbled, loudly.

Dean gave me a knowing look. "You should have eaten when we were talking to Everly."

I frowned. "It's not professional to eat a meal with a suspect."

He sighed. "Why don't you go get something to eat while I start cleaning up all this mess?" He walked down the hall to a storage closet and pulled out a vacuum and a broom.

"*Hmm*, I guess so. Are you going to be okay on your own?" I asked.

He scoffed. "Okay to do what? To clean my own house? I think I'll be all right, detective."

I rolled my eyes. "You can call me Noah."

"What?"

"My name, it's *Noah*."

Dean leaned on the broom and smiled. "Okay. Well, go eat then, Noah. I promise not to get robbed or murdered before you get back. And if anyone tries, I have a new panic door to use."

I laughed through my nose and smirked. "Thanks. I do like to try and keep my clients alive. Just an annoying habit of mine."

He chuckled. "*So* annoying."

I turned away and was about to leave when I heard Dean getting a call—his Bond ringtone being so unique. A second later he said, "Noah! Come back!"

I jogged down the hall to Dean. "What is it? What's wrong?" Did the cops want to speak to him again? Had he been threatened? No. He was grinning like a Cheshire cat.

His eyes were wide, delirious. "You're never going to guess what Felicity just told me."

"What?"

He shook his head. "You have to wait until she comes over to find out."

"You're kidding me?" He was going to withhold information just to be dramatic? "You understand that you're *paying* me to solve this case, correct?"

He nodded. "I understand completely."

We waited for fifteen *agonizing* minutes. I sat down and watched Dean clean up the lounge, righting chairs and fluffing up dusty pillows.

He'd taken off his suit jacket and slung it over the bar. All I could do was stare him down, watching his smooth muscles flex under his dress shirt as he lifted the corner of a settee to clean underneath. My pent up annoyance was quickly developing into something else. Felicity had better get here soon or I'd be doing something I'd regret later.

Why did I tell him he could call me Noah? I'd never let a client call me by my first name before. It was so unprofessional. He brought something out of me whenever he was around and I wasn't entirely sure if I was comfortable with that.

He flicked his eyes up to meet mine and gave me a lopsided smile as he righted a side table and dusted it off. He was about to plug in the vacuum when the front door opened down the hall. "Hello?" Felicity called into the space.

"In here!" Dean yelled back.

Felicity came running into the room—as fast as someone wearing heels *could* run. She'd opted for a sensible pair of jeans and a flowy top, but combined it with a set of devilishly high shoes. Her crimson lips were set in a wide grin as she looked between the two of us.

"Tell him," Dean coaxed, gesturing with his hands.

She let out a deep breath and turned to me. "I figured out who bought the cologne."

I almost fell out of my chair. "You *what*?"

She strode over and sat beside me. "I know. You thought it couldn't be done, however I know people you don't. I got the sample over to my friend who works in a high-end fragrance boutique and he knew it right off the bat. *Homme de pouvoir.*"

"Meaning?"

She grinned. "Meaning, only *one* man buys that fragrance in bulk. Teddy Lazzo."

"Teddy Lazzo?" Why did that name sound so familiar? "Shit, the *mobster*, Teddy Lazzo?"

Felicity nodded. "The one and only. Apparently he buys a bottle of this stuff for every one of his men."

I shook my head. "And we're sure this isn't a coincidence?"

Felicity hit my hand. "Yes! My guy is positive."

This changed things tremendously. Not only were we looking for a professional thief, but one that was tied to the underground crime world. "I'm...speechless."

Dean grinned. "See? I told you he would be. Amazing work, darling."

"So whoever stole the statue did so on Teddy Lazzo's orders?" I turned over the idea in my mind. Teddy Lazzo was untouchable. If *he* had the statue it was either long gone or in some deep, dark hole we'd never be able to uncover.

"It would appear so. Unless someone was acting out on their own?" Felicity suggested.

"Maybe." The room was quiet for a second while I processed the news. This story kept getting bigger and wilder. I pulled myself together and changed the subject, remembering what I wanted to ask her. "So, Felicity, what do you know about the bulky, tattooed guy you invited to the party? What was his name?"

She pinched her brows and frowned. "Oh, um, let me remember. Something Sax, Gavin or Garrett, maybe?"

"I can't help but notice that you forgot to mention him the other day when you gave us your list of guests." I hardly knew Felicity, and yet it didn't seem like something she would do—she didn't strike me as forgetful. She'd been on top of every other detail I'd asked her about. What was different about this guy?

She flushed while Dean frowned, opening his mouth to no doubt come to her defense, only she held up her hand and stopped him. "I've got this, Dean."

He closed his mouth, but didn't take his narrowed gaze off of me.

"To be perfectly frank, detective, I *didn't* forget about him."

"I had a feeling that might be the case."

She crossed her legs the other way and shifted her position on the sofa, straightening her back into a rigid position. "The only reason that I didn't mention him before was because he...scared me."

"He scared you? So why did you invite him to your party, then?" It seemed like an odd thing to do.

Dean moved across the space to sit beside Felicity and took her hand in his.

"I didn't, not exactly." She peered down at her lap. "I was at the club and he cornered me at the bar. He kept asking me what I was doing later, what my plans were. I thought if I casually brought up Dean and the party maybe he'd back off and leave me alone, only it had the *opposite* effect. I thought it would warn him off. That he'd take the hint that I wasn't interested, and I had friends who were expecting me. But then he *followed* me from the club to the house. I was freaked out." She shook her head. "I don't know how he got past the security gate."

"I see. And how did he act once he got to the party?"

She looked up to meet my eyes. "He was *fine*, actually. He stayed away from me since I was with Dean most of the night and he was the first one to leave, if I remember. Honestly, I felt silly about the whole thing, and I didn't want to bring it up. I didn't see how he could have been involved with the theft of the statue, so I thought it was reasonable to omit that detail altogether."

I could tell that she was beating herself up about it and was genuinely worried about this guy, so I treaded lightly. "Okay. Thanks for telling me the truth, Ms. Reed. I appreciate that. Although, generally, in a murder investigation, nothing should be omitted, no matter how small the detail."

She nodded, looking back down at her hand holding Dean's. They shared a few private words that were too quiet to make out.

After a beat I caught Dean's eye. "Well, I think it's safe to say that we have our next lead. If we're now looking for a mobster, I think Gavin Sax is our new main suspect."

Dean nodded. "He certainly looked like he could kill a man."

I snapped my fingers. "Speaking of that. Does this mean that our victim was one of Lazzo's men as well? He fits the profile."

Felicity pulled herself together, rolling her shoulders back. "Could be. I gather the police haven't been able to figure out who he is yet?"

I shook my head. "Nope. He's untraceable. Another red flag against him."

"Why's that?" she asked.

"Well most people are easy to find because they have nothing to hide," I explained. "People like our victim, who have no ties to the world, are suspicious."

Felicity played with a ring on her finger, a habit I was intimately familiar with. "I suppose so."

Dean quickly filled her in on what we'd found on his uncle's computer and how our suspect pool was finally beginning to shrink. She laughed. "The tricky bastard. Of course he hid the camera from you. He doesn't trust anyone, not even family."

Dean threw an arm around Felicity's shoulders and drew her in tight. "I would trust you with anything."

Her lips pulled into a smile. "I know, Dean. Me too."

A cord inside my chest was strung tight watching them together and I couldn't explain why. I cleared my throat and stood up. "I think it's time we get this show on the road; we're burning daylight and we have some people to talk to."

Dean sighed and stood up. "You're right. Let's go catch this guy." He helped Felicity to her feet and kissed her on the cheek. "We couldn't have done it without you, darling. Thanks a million."

She smiled and patted Dean's now stubbled face. "Don't mention it. Just let me know how it goes."

"I'll see you tonight."

We all left out the front door and Felicity drove away in her own car —a black eighties Mustang. I'd half expected them to have matching cars, but no, their personalities were too different. Dean was wild where Felicity was calm under pressure, logical. Even when she was describing her fear of Sax she wasn't the ball of nerves I would have expected, merely a less animated version of herself, closed off.

Dean leaped into the driver's seat of the Speedster and shouted, "Let's go, maestro!"

I rolled my eyes and climbed in beside him. "Just drive, Dean."

He laughed and started the engine. "Okay, okay. Don't be so touchy, Noah."

I smiled and tore my gaze away from him. Today was not going *at all* how I pictured it. Only, I couldn't tell if it was for the better or for the worse. We had more information now, only with more information came more questions. So many questions.

ELEVEN

"We need to stop at my office," I said as we rolled up to a line of unmoving cars.

Dean glanced my way. "Why, did you forget something?" His eyes lit up. "Are you getting your gun?"

I frowned and narrowed my eyes at him. "For your information, I don't own a gun. Unless you count a taser gun, though I think we can do without this time."

He tapped his hand on the wheel. "So...what, then?"

"I think since we're so close to this thing, we need to do more than just *interview* Sax."

"Meaning?"

I gestured casually. "We need to follow him. If we interview him he might spook. Or he'll know we're after him. I don't want to give him the upper hand, especially if he actually is working for Lazzo. I could do without a mobster on my back; it's not great for business."

Dean pulled in a quick breath and grinned like a schoolboy. "A stakeout?"

"Yes, which is why we need to go get my car," I said. "Yours sticks out like a sore thumb. Not very covert."

He bobbed his head, still grinning.

I rolled my eyes. "Stop smiling like that or I won't let you come along."

He immediately frowned. "You're such a party pooper, Noah."

I leaned back against the seat, my arm over the edge of the window. "Yeah, that's what they all tell me."

* * *

We pulled up to the office and Dean parked around back next to the dumpster where I kept my own car—a nineties black Jeep.

"So what do we need for a stakeout?" Dean asked. "Sunglasses? Trench coats? A zoom lens?"

I pointed at his face. "You're already wearing sunglasses, or did you forget?"

He smirked. "I meant more, like, *covert* sunglasses."

157

"Let me tell you something about being covert." I got out of the car and shut the door. "Being covert means going unnoticed. Trench coats and newspapers are a comedy bit *because* they're so noticeable. We don't *need* anything to follow someone, just common sense."

He deflated. "Oh, I was kinda hoping for a costume change or something."

I surveyed him. He *did* stand out in his suit and tie in the middle of the city. "I might have something you can wear if you want to change."

He looked up, his eyes alight. "Really?"

I shrugged. "Sure. I need to take Captain for a walk anyway, so we have a minute to spare."

"Captain?" he asked.

"Oh, my dog. He usually does okay on his own, although I can't leave him all day or I'll come home to a surprise, if you know what I mean."

He gave me a lopsided grin. "I didn't know you had a dog."

I laughed through my nose. "There are lots of things you don't know about me." And there were *definitely* lots of things I didn't know about Dean. There was still something strange about him. Something I couldn't quite pin down. It was more than his eagerness to butt into this investigation, more than the annoying confidence.

He smiled with his hands in his pockets. "I guess so."

I took him through the back door and up the stairs to my apartment. The whole situation was odd. I'd never brought a client into my personal space before. I thought about grabbing him some clothes so he could change using the office, but it was already locked up and this was much faster. We entered the cramped living space and I tried not to feel self-conscious over the full garbage can or the messy breakfast table covered with papers.

Captain smelled someone new immediately. He ran into the room and attacked Dean with his tongue.

Dean laughed. "Well hello to you too."

"I'll be right back," I told him as I slipped into my bedroom. Dean was a little taller than me, though roughly the same size. I grabbed an old navy-blue sweatshirt from my closet and a pair of gray khakis from my dresser. Thinking how silly that would look with his fancy dress shoes I grabbed an old pair of running shoes that Malcolm had left behind that I thought might fit. It wasn't like Malcolm was going to come back for them. I should have donated the pair months ago. I'd just never found the time, or that's what I told myself.

When I came back into the main room Dean was crouching on the floor, scratching Captain behind the ear. The black labradoodle was wagging his tail with joy. "Here you go." I handed Dean the pile. "The bathroom's over there. I'll be right back with Captain."

He smiled. "Thanks, Noah."

There was that string again, pulling taut in my stomach. "No problem." I clapped my hands. "Come on, Captain." I left Dean alone and took Captain out for a walk. We covered our usual route around the block where he marked his favorite tree—which was special and completely different from the identical tree that stood two feet away.

Being away from Dean for a minute gave me a moment to think. This case was so puzzling. Someone associated with a high-level mobster had stolen a priceless antiquity from Mr. William's house. But then why come back the next day and kill that man? The unidentified man who was possibly *also* connected to Teddy Lazzo? What had they been looking for if they'd already gotten what they wanted? It seemed pretty out of character for a career criminal to return to the scene of the crime, and to leave any sort of evidence, much less a whole murder victim. Maybe assuming the thief and the killer were the same person was incorrect, only it seemed impossible that it could be anything else. There were too many variables, too many possible suspects with dubious alibis.

Captain pulled me into a jog as we wrapped around the corner back to the office. I'd texted Lexi about our next move earlier and she's said she'd come up with nothing on Gavin Sax. He was a complete unknown. Exactly the kind of man we were looking for.

Captain beat me up the stairs and I entered the apartment after him. Dean was now dressed in my clothes. They fit almost perfectly on his frame, though as I'd suspected, the pants were slightly too short, brushing his ankles. "Did the shoes fit?"

He wiggled his foot. "Like a glove. Who knew we'd be the same shoe size?"

"Oh, we're not." I shrugged. "Those are just leftover from... someone else."

He nodded, knowingly. "Ah, I see."

I unclipped Captain's lead and he ran off to my bedroom to lay down. "Ready?" I asked.

Dean put on a smile, breaking the tension. "Yep, let's go be covert."

I locked up the office again and ran ahead of Dean to start the car. It was great to finally be in the driver's seat after so many days of being a passenger. I gripped the steering wheel and let out a breath.

"Was my driving actually that bad?" Dean asked as he slipped into the passenger seat beside me, noticing my contentment.

"God, yes. You should be stripped of your license."

He scoffed. "Gee, tell me how you really feel, why don't you?"

"Sorry, but you should be lucky I'm not a cop," I said. "How many tickets do you currently have?"

He clicked on his seat belt. "None..." he grinned, "...right now anyway."

I laughed as I put the car in drive and pulled out of the lot. The only thing Lexi had managed to find on Sax was a home address. Thank God for public records. It was near Hollywood, although not the nice side—an apartment with dozens of identical units. I pulled up along the opposite curb and parked.

"So what now?" Dean asked, his eyes narrowed on the apartment building. He'd started sucking on a toothpick like he was a cop in an old movie or something. *Where the hell did he even get that?*

I plucked the toothpick from his mouth and threw it out the open window.

He drew back, his brow furrowed. "Hey!"

"Now," I crossed my arms, "we wait."

Dean mirrored me and slumped down in his seat. "Wait for what?"

"For Sax, obviously."

The address Lexi had found online didn't have the exact unit number, which meant we'd have to sit around and wait for him to come or go. It wasn't a great strategy. Unfortunately, it was all what we had to work with despite our new information.

Ten minutes passed in silence before Dean got bored. "This sucks," he blurted out, bursting the bubble of quiet in the car.

"*This* is detective work," I reminded him. "You can go home any time you want, Dean."

He laughed. "And miss all the action?"

Another few silent minutes passed. I was keenly aware of how physically close we were. Dean's arm brushed mine as he shifted in his seat.

He leaned back and pulled one foot up onto the dash. "So what's up with shoe guy?"

I glanced over at him. "*What?*"

"You used to have a partner at the agency, didn't you?"

Had Lexi mentioned something? No. She wouldn't have.

I averted my eyes. "A long time ago. How did you know?"

He shrugged. "Your office. I could tell there used to be two work spaces, and then you'd moved your desk to the center—there were indents on the carpet. So it couldn't have been *that* long ago."

God, why was he so perceptive? And why was he choosing *now* to bring it up? I locked my eyes on the apartment building, determined not to lose our lead. "Okay."

"*Okay?* What does that mean?"

"It means, what do you want me to say?"

Dean shifted. "I don't know. I was curious. He was a work partner, but you had his shoes in your apartment, so...he was also more than that?"

I let out a deep sigh. I hadn't talked to anyone about Malcolm. My parents knew, although they were happy to see him leave. In their eyes he was the reasonable one and they hoped his leaving would finally knock some sense into me and send me running back to law school. Lexi knew as well, only we didn't talk about it. My teenage niece had better things to do than listen to her uncle trauma dump about his failed relationship.

163

"He was...more than that." I shook my head. "But it didn't work out."

After a beat he asked, "How come?"

I turned towards him and tried to read his expression. "Are you really asking?" Why did he want to know?

He shrugged. "Yeah, I am." He seemed genuine, his lips pressed into a small, disarming smile.

I let out a breath, thinking over the last year. How could I explain it simply? "He said I worked too much, that I got lost in my cases and couldn't let things go. That I didn't spend enough time with him, outside of work, I mean."

Dean hummed into the silence. "And was he right?"

I caught his eye and held it for a second too long. *Was he right?* "Maybe." How was he ballsy enough to ask such a personal question? And why had I answered it?

"Relationships are hard," he said, "for anyone, much less a detective. That's why I don't hold on to people long enough for them to grow resentful."

Huh, I wondered how he explained his relationship with Felicity? It seemed like they'd known each other for years. What made her different?

Dean interrupted my scattered thoughts. "Is that him?" he asked, pointing toward the street.

I hit his side. "Don't point, genius."

He jerked his hand back and slumped further into the seat. *Very inconspicuous.*

I gazed over and caught sight of our guy walking down the street away from his apartment. He was big and tall with tattoos on his neck and hands. A long coat covered the rest of him, but I was sure he was tattooed everywhere else too. He was bald up top with a scruffy, dark beard.

"That's him," I said calmly.

Dean slapped the dash, his eyes wide. "Okay, start the car."

I turned. "Dean, chill out. You have to give a subject some lead time unless you want to spook them. This isn't a movie," I reminded him.

"But he's getting away," Dean whined.

"No. He's not. I can see him perfectly in my rearview mirror. He's on foot, so he's not going far. We need to ditch the Jeep."

"What? I thought the whole point of the car was to be covert? Won't he spot us?"

"Well he doesn't know what *I* look like, does he? You better stay in the car."

He snorted. "Yeah, right."

I sighed and grabbed a blue baseball cap from the glove box and shoved it on his head, no doubt ruining his hair. "Stay ten feet away from me. We don't know each other, got it?"

"Fine," he huffed out.

"If I lose him we'll split up." I hopped out of the car and straightened my jacket.

"Roger that."

I rolled my eyes and started walking, keeping Sax at least a hundred feet in front of me. Dean did as instructed and stayed far away. When we turned the corner our suspect had crossed the street. I motioned for Dean to stay on the right as I followed Sax. Hollywood melted into West Hollywood and we entered an area filled with bars and nightclubs.

What was Sax doing in West Hollywood? Surely Lazzo wasn't hanging out at a gay bar in the middle of the day, was he? It was barely scraping three o'clock. Maybe Sax was meeting with a seller for the statue in some back alley?

After a few minutes of walking he stopped in front of a nondescript beige building and slipped inside. There was no sign on the outside. No way of knowing where he'd entered. It could be anything.

I stopped a ways away and let Dean catch up with me. "Where'd he go?" he asked with a heavy breath.

"He went inside there."

"Are we following?"

"*Hmm*, it could be dangerous." I weighed the options. "We don't know what we're getting into."

Dean blew out a sharp breath. "It's probably just a club. We're in West Hollywood, after all."

166

I had to admit I didn't know much about the club scene. I'd only ever been to a couple bars with Malcolm and they were never hidden in plain sight like this one. It worried me.

"I'll go first, then." Dean strode forward.

I bit my tongue and followed my sidekick down the pavement to the building. It appeared like it had been a storefront at one time, however both windows had been bricked over and painted the same shade of beige. The door was solid wood and didn't match the building, clearly a new addition. "Do I knock?" Dean asked right as the door opened in front of him.

A man in a pinstripe suit smiled with bleach-white teeth and beckoned us inside. "Come in, gentlemen."

Dean gave me a wary look before following inside. I hesitated before crossing the threshold, suddenly regretful that I hadn't brought my taser, Tasha. We walked down a short set of stairs to a cramped, dark hallway with small wall sconces providing barely enough light to see in front of us.

"Who are you gentlemen here to see today?" the man asked with an intense stare, his eyes boring into us.

"Uh..." Dean and I looked at each other in confusion.

"Gavin Sax?" I offered, because what the hell else was I supposed to say?

The man lowered his voice and leaned in. "We don't use government names here, gentlemen. Is this your first time at Fantasma?"

Dean smiled brightly. "Yes, sorry. Still learning the rules."

"I'm sure Saxon would be more than happy for a walk-in. Right this way, gentlemen."

He turned and passed in front of us. I caught Dean's eye and he shrugged. What the hell were we in for? Was Sax meeting Lazzo here? Or something else entirely? And why was he using an alter ego?

The man in the striped suit opened a door at the end of the hallway that blended right into the dark walls; I'd almost missed it. "Saxon will give you the appropriate paperwork to sign. All our hosts are independent contractors and conduct themselves accordingly."

Hosts? What exactly was he hosting?

Dean grinned, his hands clasped behind his back. "Thanks."

We slipped into the room and the door was closed behind us. The space was small and dark with a black Chesterfield sofa on one side and a tall red standing partition on the other.

"What the hell is this?" I whispered beside Dean's ear.

He beamed with wide eyes and hit my shoulder. "I have no idea, but I'm excited to find out."

And find out we did.

Gavin Sax came out from behind the partition, only he was dressed completely different than he had been ten minutes ago. Gone were the pants and the coat and in their place was a black leather jock strap, a matching leather vest, and a little black motorcycle cap straight out of the eighties.

"Gentlemen, hello..." he stopped whatever speech he'd prepared when he caught sight of Dean. "Oh. *I* know you."

Dean waved. "Hi, uh, nice to see you again?"

Sax smirked. "Have you brought a friend along for some fun?"

I took a step back instinctively. "And what kind of fun is that, exactly?"

He reached behind the partition and I automatically stepped in front of Dean thinking he was pulling a gun. What he actually grabbed was much worse. A leather riding crop. *Oh.* Shit.

Dean laughed and stepped out from behind me. "No, no, we're not here for that. We're here for something *entirely* different."

Sax's face dropped. "Oh?"

"We're here about the party on Friday night," I got out, finding my voice. I wasn't a *prude*, however I was wholly unprepared for whatever was happening in this room.

"Yeah, about that. Sorry I left so abruptly. I was under the false impression that your party was going to be more up my alley."

Dean crossed his arms. "*Ah.*"

"Yeah, when your friend invited me at the club I was there visiting a client, and I thought she was asking for a similar service, if you know what I mean."

Dean nodded. "Well I do *now*. I think maybe there was some confusion on *both* sides. You scared my friend."

His face fell. "I scared her? I'm sorry, that was *not* my intention. I thought she was playing along with me. I guess I read the vibes wrong."

"Quite," Dean said.

So at least *that* was explained. "So you're a...what, exactly?" I asked.

Sax smiled wickedly, recovering his composure. "I'm whatever you want me to be."

"He's a *dom*," Dean explained, as if it was obvious.

Gavin put his hands on his hips and rocked on his heels. His outfit was *very* distracting. "That's one word for it. I like to think of myself as someone who can provide whatever a client needs for emotional stimulation."

I shook my head. "So you going to the party on Friday was a total misunderstanding?"

He shrugged. "The catering was nice, but yes. After I realized there'd been a miscommunication I decided to leave early. No sense in souring the party."

"So what were you doing in the back hallways at midnight?" I decided to be direct. I didn't want to hang around longer than needed. A blush crept up my neck and my shirt started to stick to my chest with heat. This was *so* not my scene.

Dean looked me up and down, no doubt noticing my distress, and raised an eyebrow.

"To be honest, I was looking for a second exit. I didn't want to be rude and leave out the front, so I slipped out the door off the kitchen."

"*Hmm*, an Irish exit, huh?" His story more or less checked out. Unless we wanted to jump to the conclusion that Lazzo was hiring *doms* to rob millionaire's mansions. It *would* be an excellent cover, however I was left unconvinced. He seemed genuine. I'd interviewed a lot of liars and Gavin Sax wasn't one of them.

"And out of curiosity, do you remember where you were yesterday morning between eight and nine?" I asked.

He shrugged. "I was here, working."

Dean smiled and asked, "Do you get a lot of early morning clients?"

Dean was having *way* too much fun for my comfort.

Sax nodded. "Yeah, a lot of my regulars come in before work to release some tension.

"Oh I *bet* they do," Dean replied with a smirk.

"*Okay*, well, thank you for your time. If we have any more questions we'll contact you."

"You sure you don't want to stay for a session?" he asked, slapping the riding crop against his open palm.

171

"We're good," I said at the same time as Dean said, "Maybe another time."

I couldn't get out of there fast enough. I didn't even look back to see if Dean was following behind me before bursting out the front doors onto the West Hollywood sidewalk. I breathed in a lungful of fresh LA smog. Something about that place made me claustrophobic—my skin was tingling with electricity.

"Well that was wild," Dean said behind me. "You okay?"

I turned and nodded, pulling myself together. "Of course I'm okay. Just disappointed that lead was a bust."

He shrugged. "It narrows down our suspect pool, right? Gavin Sax had opportunity, but no motive, and as far as we know no ties to Lazzo or the crime world."

"*As far as we know,*" I repeated. This case was not going at all how I'd planned. A full two days in and we hardly had any solid leads. Everything was wishy-washy.

"So who is off our list so far?" Dean asked. "Conrad?"

I nodded and started walking down the block. Dean jogged to keep up. "Yeah, no way Conrad was involved. He has no motive—he doesn't need money, and even though he had opportunity he was on the other side of the house stealing that pen from the library. Of course that could all be a ruse if he was working with a partner or trying to throw us off the trail, however I don't think it was."

172

We reached the Jeep and I jumped into the driver's seat.

"I agree," Dean said, sliding into the car. "Frankly, I don't think Tyler Conrad is smart enough to pull something like that off. And we already know that MIT was a fluke. Even if he was working with someone, he'd have to understand the security system and how to get the statue out at the end of the night. That's what I keep coming back to. Yeah, I might have been drinking during the party, but I feel like I would have noticed someone carrying a large package with them when they left.

"*Hmm*, you have a point. If they *were* working with a partner—maybe our dead guy—they could have handed it off to someone else during the party. Or possibly through the kitchen side door that Sax was talking about? If the alarm was off, that door wouldn't have been a problem for them."

"I guess anybody who was wandering around in the halls could have passed it off without being seen. That stupid camera conveniently didn't cover the proper angle above the study door."

I agreed, the camera was peculiar. "They probably knew about the camera and moved it slightly," I argued. "It's less suspicious than turning it off or smashing it."

"So they *knew* they'd be seen?"

I nodded. "Or their partner."

I started the Jeep and pulled off the curb. My stomach growled.

Dean's eyes went wide. "Oh shit, you never got to eat lunch, did you?" he asked, his face full of parental concern.

I waved my hand. "I'm fine. We should interview the next guy, Hackney or whatever he's called."

Dean frowned. "I insist that you eat something. It's not good to sleuth on an empty stomach."

I rolled my eyes, and then my stomach grumbled again, louder this time. "Fine, we can work on our suspect list while I eat." I turned around the corner to the right, directing the car back toward my side of town.

* * *

I pulled into the Greta's Diner parking lot and we entered the establishment. I was positive Dean was used to upscale coffeehouses and restaurants, but he didn't seem fazed as we walked in. Rosalie seated us with her usual bored demeanor and handed Dean a menu. I didn't need one; I'd memorized the single page of offerings.

"So who else can we take off our list of suspects?" he asked as he scanned the laminated page.

"Mrs. Wong, for sure," I replied. "There's a small chance that she could be working with someone else—she does have motive, though no real opportunity."

He set down the menu. "She wasn't on the video."

"Correct, and your friend Felicity confirmed that she was in the lounge during the time the statue was stolen."

"So no Conrad, no Mrs. Wong. What about Everly?"

I shook my head. "The makeup influencer? Do you think Lazzo is hiring skinny beauty queens to steal priceless statues and kill anyone that gets in their way? Besides, she doesn't have the skills or the knowledge needed for this level of crime. "

He shrugged. "You're probably right. I think she just desperately wanted some investors for her company. I don't think she gave off killer vibes. What about Miguel? He was on the video and his alibi is weak."

"That's true. We definitely need to revisit Miguel. He had opportunity, he had motive—funding his social media lifestyle—and he's young."

Dean furrowed his brow and played with the watch on his wrist. "What does that have to do with anything?"

"Like I said before, young people do stupid things, Dean," I explained. "He might not have even known who Lazzo was and got roped into this whole situation."

"*Hmm*, maybe." He didn't sound convinced.

Rosalie came back to take our order. I got a ham and tomato on rye and Dean asked for a short stack of pancakes.

"Pancakes?" I said. "At three in the afternoon?"

He shrugged. "I like diner pancakes. They're superior."

That was surprising. "I didn't realize you *went* to diners. Doesn't your crowd usually eat at places where you need a reservation?"

He shrugged, unfazed. "I like those places too, but nothing beats a fluffy pancake the size of a dinner plate."

"Hmm." Maybe some of my assumptions about him were wrong. He wasn't stuck-up like a lot of trust fund kids, he was just annoying. And annoyingly outgoing. Nothing like me.

Dean went on, "So we don't think it's either of the servers, right? Unless the whole having sex in the closet was a ruse."

I smiled, remembering yesterday morning. "Well if it was a ruse, that would make Everly and Max complicit since we have two eyewitnesses."

He frowned. "Oh yeah, I forgot about that. So they're off the list. What about Max? He seemed pretty handy with that knife."

I drummed my fingers against the table and hummed. "I'm not sure about him yet. The two servers described him as a drunk, however that's easy to fake. It could be a cover. *And* he was caught on the video, so we know he left the kitchen at least once during the party."

"That's true. So, who's left?" he asked. "Mr. Hackney?"

I nodded. "He's the only one we haven't talked to yet. Sure, he wasn't on the video, but that doesn't mean that he wasn't involved somehow. You said you were talking with him for most of the night?"

He nodded. "Yeah, a large portion of it, though what kind of host would I be if I ignored my other guests? There were definitely moments when he was gone and I didn't know where he was. I hadn't given it a second thought at the time, of course."

176

"Right. So he might have had an opportunity, only what's his motive? Didn't you say he was rich?"

Dean nodded. "Mr. Hackney is a *tremendously* wealthy man. I find it hard to believe that he would stoop to stealing a statue for a mob boss. Unless he was in deep with them and he was being forced to act. I don't know him well enough to say."

"We'll ask when we see him, won't we?" I texted Lexi and asked her to give us anything she could find on Hackney, including where he was today. Rich men like him were often hard to track down, however we'd been getting lucky lately, catching people off guard when they least expected it. Or maybe it wasn't luck. Dean had pulled more than a few strings. Where would I be in this investigation without him?

Rosalie brought us our meals and we ate quickly. I was used to eating fast, working so much, only Dean took it as some sort of a challenge. He was cutting pieces off his stack of pancakes and shoving them into his mouth faster than I could keep up.

I chuckled. "You're going to make yourself sick, Dean."

"We're on a hunt for *justice*," he said through a full mouth. "Justice waits for no man."

"I think you're mixing a couple phrases there, but I get what you mean. Still, if you puke in my car, I'll have to kill you."

He gulped down his bite and smiled. "Understood."

TWELVE

After finishing lunch I got a text from Lexi.

>   **L: Hackney will be at the Hollywood Golf Club at four.**

>   **N: How'd you find that out?**

>   **L: I have my ways. Don't cross me ;)**

>   **N: Wouldn't dream of it. Thanks Lexi.**

"We have a new lead."

Dean dropped his napkin on top of his empty plate. "We do?"

"Hackney is currently playing golf right now. Can you get us in?" I asked. This interview hinged on him having another miraculous contact.

He laughed through his nose. "Of course I can."

I crossed my arms over my now full belly that was stuffed with fries. "Who do you know this time?"

He pushed his plate forward and took a sip of his water. "Nobody, detective."

I raised an eyebrow. "So how are you getting us in?"

He smiled, his hands laced together in front of him. "Simple. I'm a member."

I stopped myself from rolling my eyes. "Of course you are."

"Right, so let's go." He stood up to leave and before I could tell what was happening Dean had already paid the check.

I frowned and clenched my hand into a fist. "I can pay for my own meal, Dean. I'm not *that* poor."

He glanced back at me. "Who said you were poor?"

I went on. "I'm not used to people buying me things and you keep doing it." The situation was making me a little uncomfortable—the cologne, the coffee, and now a meal? He was my client, and he was supposed to be paying me for my *services*, not extras like that.

"Relax, Noah." He waved his hand and grinned. "It's not a big deal."

"To you," I replied, slipping my jacket back on.

"Okay, I'm sorry. I won't buy you any more things. I promise." He grinned in a way that led me to think he was lying, but I dropped the subject.

"Whatever, let's get going before Hackney decides to leave."

Dean didn't seem in any hurry. "The Hollywood Green has twenty holes. We've got time. Besides, we need to change."

"Change?"

He gestured to himself. "Well I can't exactly get into the club wearing these khakis, now can I? They have a dress code."

"Of course they do." What had I been thinking? "Let's be quick, then."

We hopped in the Jeep and drove down the block to the office. "Okay, you have five minutes," I told him. "I'm gonna take Captain out and you better be dressed when I get back."

Dean smirked. "Or what, detective? You'll arrest me?"

I rolled my eyes and clapped my hands for Captain to follow me. Once we reached the bottom of the stairs I realized I'd forgotten his lead. "Stay right here, boy." I jogged up the steps and opened the door to my apartment without thinking about it, and I caught Dean in a state of half-undress. He was shirtless, but he'd already slipped on his trousers. His pale torso was smooth and bare except for a beeline of dark hair that ran down from his navel into his waistband. He clearly worked out as proven by his broad shoulders and toned stomach. He probably had a private trainer like every other rich kid in Hollywood. "Sorry, I forgot his leash." Heat crept up the back of my neck as I avoided looking at him to grab the lead off the wall.

"It's okay." He smiled, putting his hands on his hips. "Though, It's a good thing you didn't catch me with my pants down because I'm wearing *super* embarrassing gnome underwear that Felicity got me for Christmas."

My mind went blank and words escaped me. All I could think about was what Dean looked like under those trousers with his funny gnome underwear, which made me blush even more. "Uh...bye." I slipped out the door and raced downstairs to the waiting Captain. "Well *that* was awkward," I mumbled to myself.

I took Captain out to the back of the building where there was a little grass for him to relieve himself. When I came back, Dean was fully clothed in his gray suit again.

"Dressed?" I asked, even though I could see for myself that he was.

He smiled confidently. "Yep." He seemed to be amused by my distress, the sadist.

"Okay, then." I sent Captain off to my room and was about to leave when Dean stopped me with an outstretched hand on my chest. I could feel his warmth through my thin t-shirt. I tore my head up in surprise. "What—"

"You need a suit jacket," he said, as if it was obvious.

I glanced down at my outfit and frowned. "I do?"

"They won't let you in otherwise. He scrutinized me. "Do you... have one?"

I narrowed my eyes. "*Yes, I have one.* Give me a second." I went to my bedroom and riffled through the back of my closet. I knew there was at least a single jacket in there. I tore off my leather jacket and slipped the new one on. I walked back out to the main room for Dean's approval."

He smiled, looking at the new outfit. "Nice, though you do know wearing black and navy together is a fashion no-no, right?"

I gave him a withering look. "Arrest me. Will it get us in?"

He cocked his head to the side and appraised me again. "Yes, I think so."

"Then it's good enough. Let's go. We're already running behind."

"Bye, Captain," Dean said behind me as I closed the door.

I stopped beside the Jeep, however Dean kept walking until he stood beside his own car. "What?" he said, "We're not undercover anymore, remember?"

I sighed and walked over to get in the passenger seat of the Speedster. "Fine, but only because it will blend in better with the other rich-guy cars."

Dean nodded. "Of course."

* * *

Dean drove us across town to the golf course. Only it was more than just a golf course, it was an expensive country club too. The building was white sandstone with columns and lattice windows that made me feel poor just looking at them. Dean pulled his car around to the front, which was covered by a gold awning, and stopped. He automatically got out and handed the nearest valet a few bills. I pinched my brows as he gave the man his keys and I followed after him.

He turned and noticed my displeasure. "I didn't buy you anything! That was for *my* sake, not yours."

"*Uh-huh*," I replied, not convinced at all.

He shrugged. "If you're going to get mad about money all the time you're *really* not going to like this next part."

I jogged to catch up to him. "What do you mean?"

We entered the lobby of the clubhouse through a set of heavy glass doors. The stone floor was covered in plush, blue velvet carpet and the walls were lacquered with gold accents.

The older man behind the front desk seemed to recognize Dean. I wondered if they were required to memorize all of their premium members. "Mr. Prescott, nice to see you again. Here for a round?"

Dean smiled his usual toothpaste-ad grin. "Yep, and I've brought a guest, so I'll need a guest pass too."

The man smiled. "Of course, give me one moment."

Dean turned back to me. "We'll need to get access to the golf course in order to speak to Mr. Hackney. I'm sure he has his people with him."

I crossed my arms. "Why do rich people always have a group with them at all times?"

He shrugged. "Safety, mostly. Some rich people make a lot of enemies."

183

"Do you have enemies?" I asked, genuinely curious. He didn't strike me as the type to have *true* enemies, though he was annoying enough.

He grinned, his dark brown eyes gazing directly into mine. "Maybe."

I turned away first. "Well let's hope that none of them are here today."

Dean laughed and turned back to the front desk where he was handed a lanyard and a keycard. He gave the lanyard to me and slipped the keycard into his pocket. "Thanks, Gerrard."

The man beamed with pride. "Any time, Mr. Prescott."

I wondered how many members actually remembered *his* name.

"Come on, let's get on the course, Noah."

I pulled the lanyard over my head and followed Dean down the hallway toward the restaurant at the back of the club. I glanced at the plastic card hanging at my chest. "So how much did this guest pass set you back?"

He turned to catch my eye and grinned. "Do you really want to know?"

I shook my head, changing my mind. "No, I just decided I don't. I'm going to pretend it was free."

"It's actually quite a sweet deal, Noah. You can even get in the sauna when we're done if you'd like," he said, pointing down a hallway to the right.

I laughed through my nose. "Something tells me we're not going to have time for that, unfortunately."

He cocked his head to the side and sucked on his teeth. "You're probably right."

We went out a glass door that led to the outside seating area for the restaurant. It was elevated and looked over the golf course, which was expansive. "How are we going to find him?" I asked, gazing across the swath of green. How much precious water did it take to keep it so luscious?

"Easy, come on." Dean gestured to follow him down the stairs to the right toward the course. We passed a small storage shed with golf carts lined up beside it. There were a couple young guys standing around in their golf attire. They seemed barely old enough to be in college. Dean said something to one of them that I didn't hear and slipped him some bills. I clenched my jaw knowing how much money Dean was wasting on this investigation, even more annoyed by its effectiveness.

He jogged back to me. "Mr. Hackney is already on the tenth hole, so we're better off driving than walking."

"Do you just pay everyone for everything?" I asked without thinking about how rude that sounded.

He smirked, his dark eyes turning honey in the golden light. "Not everything, detective."

Was he flirting with me? We didn't have time for this. "Do you know how to drive one of these things?" I gestured toward the golf cart.

"Of course." He hopped in the driver's seat. "Jump in, Noah. Daylight is burning."

I slipped into the seat and Dean immediately slammed on the gas pedal, rocketing us forward. I gripped the bar above my head tightly to stay on. "Jesus, you're even more of a menace *off* the road," I mumbled.

He turned. "What?"

"*Nothing.*" I smiled brightly.

We made good time across the course, following the winding gravel trail through the greens.

"There he is." Dean pointed in front of us. "And he's not alone." The two men were standing at the top of a hill where a flag stood for the end of a green. The shorter of the two men—who I was assuming was Mr. Hackney based on his golfing outfit—was choosing a new club from his golf bag. The taller one wore a serious expression and was dressed in a ruffled black suit—clearly security.

"What's the plan?" Dean asked as we got closer.

I shrugged. "You're the one that knows the guy."

He pulled in a breath through his teeth. "Yeah, that's what I'm worried about."

I turned to catch his gaze. "What do you mean?"

"*Nothing.* Here we go." He rolled the golf cart to a stop at the base of the hill and we climbed the rest of the way. Mr. Hackney and his associate didn't look pleased to be interrupted.

"Mr. Hackney?" Dean asked in faux surprise. "I *thought* that was you. Good to see you."

Mr. Hackney narrowed his eyes. "I would say the same, Mr. Prescott, only it's *not* nice to see you. I thought we had a deal?"

What was I walking into here?

Dean smiled genially. "We did, we did. Only things got a little complicated on my end and I had to take a step back for a moment. You understand."

He did *not* look like he understood. "*Hmm.*"

"It's a good thing that I caught you because I was actually going to call you today anyway. It seems that something was taken from my uncle's study during the party Friday night."

His face turned a shade darker. "And you think *I* stole it? You don't honor your deal and now you're calling me a thief?"

Dean didn't seem worried about the escalation. He grinned and said, "No, not at all. I *know* that you didn't do it, you were with me most of the night. I was only wondering if you saw anyone *else* being suspect."

Mr. Hackney straightened up and leaned against his golf club. He was wearing a dress shirt under a navy quarter-zip with ostentatious diamond cufflinks, a gold watch, and a newsboy cap covering his, no doubt, bald head. "Really?" He relaxed a fraction.

Dean put his hands in his suit jacket pockets. "Yes."

Hackney cocked his head back in thought. "There was that upstart little Latin boy that seemed pretty suspicious. He kept wandering around drinking up all the scotch."

I turned to Dean and subtly mouthed *Latin boy?*

Dean clenched his jaw. "Thanks for the information. Anything else?"

"Hmm, there was that Black girl, not your friend, the fat one who was serving the champagne. She was acting pretty suspicious too."

Wow, okay.

"We'll keep that in mind, thanks."

I could tell Dean was restraining himself from saying what he *really* wanted to say, what *I* really wanted to say.

"Just out of curiosity, what were you doing Saturday morning?" I asked, even though I wanted this conversation to be over. We still needed his alibi for the murder.

He raised an eyebrow. "Why do you want to know?"

I waved my hand. "We're asking everyone, standard procedure."

"And you are?" he asked with narrowed eyes, as if only just realizing I was there too.

"Noah Sun, private detective. Mr. Prescott has hired me to help him find his lost item."

"*Huh.*" He paused for a few seconds, analyzing me, and then relented. "Saturday morning?" He thought about it for a moment before he said, "I was down in Orange County at the grand opening of a new store. Does that satisfy you?"

I nodded. "Okay, thanks."

He turned back to his golf clubs. "Once you clear things up, call my office, Mr. Prescott. We'll talk business."

"Will do," Dean said in a way that meant he would *not* be doing that. "Thanks for answering our questions. Good luck on the course. I hear number eleven is a real bitch—sand trap."

Mr. Hackney chuckled and waved us off as we walked away.

"What a racist prick," Dean said as soon as we were out of earshot.

I nodded in agreement. "Yeah, I'd say so."

"Now I'm glad that I didn't do business with him. I hadn't realized he was *that* type of asshole." He jumped into the golf cart and I sat on the other side.

"Not to mention that he wasn't helpful at all," I argued. "Cherry had an alibi and we already knew about Miguel."

"Yeah, we were going to talk to Miguel again anyway. You don't think that Hackney could be trying to cover for himself could he?"

"*Hmm.*" I thought it over. "I can see how it's possible he's tied to the mob. He has a whole chain of hardware stores. He could easily launder money for them. But what's the motive?"

Dean shrugged. "Good old fashioned greed? He jumped on my offer on Friday when he thought it was going to make him a lot of money, even though it could have been a pretty risky move."

"So maybe he had motive, but no opportunity. You said it yourself, he was with you and Felicity most of the night, and he wasn't on the camera, so he wasn't in the back hallway during the theft."

"*Ugh*, why couldn't it be him?" Dean screwed up his nose. "That would have been nice."

I laughed. "Agreed."

The sun was starting to dip lower in the sky as we returned the golf cart to the shed for the caddies, the sky a wash of gold and pink.

When we walked back through the clubhouse Dean said, "Are you sure you don't want to try the sauna? You can even get a free massage."

I smiled and shook my head. "I'm good. I want out of this suit." I rolled my shoulders. The ill-fitting suit jacket was pinching my armpits.

"You need my tailor," Dean threw out casually. "He's the best in the business."

"I don't imagine I'll be wearing many suits in the future." In fact, I'd probably be avoiding it.

He laughed through his nose. "That's your problem, Noah. If you want more rich clients you have to hang out where the rich clients are. Most of them require a suit."

Annoyance flared up in my chest. Why was he trying to tell me how to run my business? "I don't want to go anywhere where someone tells me how I have to dress."

"That's just life, Noah. We're constantly doing things we don't want to do in order to play the game."

I raised an eyebrow. "What have *you* sacrificed to play?" I said, feeling snarky.

He turned, all the fun-loving playfulness gone from his face. "A lot, Noah. More than you know."

Shit.

He turned back and walked ahead of me out to the parking lot. The valet was currently chatting up a petite blonde in a tennis skirt. He didn't notice us until Dean placed money in his open hand. The valet startled. "Sorry, uh..." He gazed out at the lot, jerking his head back and forth.

Dean held up his hand. "I can find it myself, thanks."

The valet shrugged and held out Dean's keys from the key locker, eager to get back to flirting.

Was Dean trying to make a point to me or something? As if *valet service* was the root of all his privileges?

I followed a few paces behind until he found the Speedster on the far side of the lot. It was all by itself in an empty row of spaces. The valet probably didn't want to risk dinging the paint job. Smart man.

"So are we interviewing Miguel again tonight?" he asked as he slipped into the driver's seat.

"Maybe. We got lucky the first time. It'll probably be harder to track him down now."

"You think he'll avoid us?"

I slid into the passenger seat. "Possibly. It depends on how closely he's following the case."

"Following the case?"

"Suspects always get antsy after being interviewed, he's probably waiting for us to..." I trailed off as a noise caught my attention. A familiar beeping that was quickly speeding up. "Get out of the car," I said, my hands clenched.

Dean pinched his brows. "*What?*"

"GET OUT OF THE CAR!" I shoved Dean through the still open driver's side door and jumped over the passenger side. We sprinted maybe ten feet behind the car before the Speedster exploded in a wave of heat and golden flames. The force of the blast threw us to the ground, Dean landing on top of me. My ears were ringing and I couldn't process what Dean was saying for a minute until the words came into focus.

"*Dammit.* What the hell was that?"

I tried to shift my upper body and my shoulder screamed in pain. "*Shit.*" My head was pounding and my vision was blurry. The Speedster was still on fire, the baby-blue paint crisped around the edges. Someone was running over from across the parking lot, then another.

"Are you okay?" Dean asked after rolling off of me.

The weight off my chest pulled me into a coughing fit. "Peachy," I got out.

"What the hell happened?" Dean's hair was all messed up from the fall. His usually crafted brown locks were fringing his forehead. "It wasn't the car, right?"

I shook my head. "No, it definitely wasn't the car." Someone had just tried to kill us. And I was royally pissed off.

THIRTEEN

Dean sat up on the pavement, his palms covered in small cuts and dirt. "How did you even know?" he asked.

I pinched my eyes shut and wiggled my fingers to make sure they were still working. "I watch a lot of war movies."

Dean laughed, almost hysterically. "What? A stupid movie just saved our hides?"

I nodded. "We owe our lives to Hollywood."

"Are you guys okay?" a squeaky voice asked.

I opened my eyes again and found the valet from before standing beside us. He couldn't have been more than eighteen; his face was flushed from running over.

"Couldn't be better," I said as I attempted to pull myself up. My back and ribs burned with every movement. That was gonna bruise for sure. I'd probably have another Dean-shaped bruise on my front side as well.

"I called the cops," he said nervously. "They should be here with an ambulance any second."

I pulled my lips down and shook my head. "Nah, we're fine. Right, Dean?" I asked. After all, *he* was the one who'd gotten the pillowy landing.

He made a show of feeling all over his body with his hands. "All my parts are intact. I think I'll be okay. *My car on the other hand.*"

The Speedster was *definitely* toast.

"Someone really doesn't want us to solve this case."

Dean nodded. "That must mean we're getting close."

His resolve was surprising. I'd imagined he was going to freak out, call the whole thing off, but if it was possible, he looked even more determined, more invigorated.

Dean glanced up at the valet and smiled. "Don't look so scared, kid. I'm not going to sue anybody."

That didn't seem to put him at ease. If anything he looked worse, as if he hadn't thought that far ahead yet. "I didn't see anybody messing with your car, Mr. Prescott. Promise."

I felt a tad silly sitting on the ground, so I forced myself up on one knee and then to a shaky standing position. "Well *someone* messed with the car." The valet wouldn't have noticed *anyone* walking past the way he was focusing all his attention on that blonde girl's assets.

Sirens grew louder as they approached. They'd made good time. I wondered if the prestige of the country club factored in at all.

Dean popped up and grabbed my arm to steady me. He leaned in. "Do you think they did it here or at your office while we were gone?"

I smiled. "If they had done it back at the office I don't think we would've made it all the way here to the golf course. Besides, I have cameras facing the rear of the building. They would have been caught, and they probably knew that. We're dealing with a professional of some kind.

He nodded. "That makes sense."

"Though I'm wondering if *this* place has cameras." I looked out across the lot and quickly spotted two at the top of a lamp post. Had our arson known they were there? Like the camera in the hallway before?

The sirens cut off as an ambulance entered the parking lot, closely followed by two cop cars. "Here we go. This should be fun." I leaned in close to Dean's ear. "Keep it vague. We don't need the cops knowing what we were doing here. We were playing golf, got it?"

He smiled, a smudge of dirt on his forehead. "I beat you by three strokes."

I laughed and immediately regretted it as my ribs screamed. Definitely bruised.

"Shit, look!" Dean pointed towards the burning car—which had mostly died down now. I almost missed what he was pointing at until he let go of me and raced over to grab it.

"What is it?" I asked when he came back. He held it out. A watch.

I dropped my jaw. "Did they actually leave their watch behind at the scene of a potential double murder?" It seemed unlikely. Had we gotten lucky? Or played for fools?

"I don't know." Dean slipped the watch into his pocket as the swarm of cops and EMTs jogged over to us.

"Smile for the camera," I whispered.

* * *

We spent over an hour talking with the cops and getting our wounds checked out. The EMTs wanted to cart us off to the hospital but both Dean and I refused. He'd gotten the better end of the deal with hardly a bruise. I, on the other hand, had bruising all over my chest and back with scrapes and cuts on my hands, face, and shins. I was sitting shirtless with my legs hanging over the back of the ambulance while the cops asked me questions. I showed them my ID and my detective license, while giving them as little information as I could manage.

I was sure they'd be telling Warner about what happened. Not because he gave a shit if *I* got hurt, but because Dean was there too. Someone had robbed his house and left a dead body in his foyer, now someone was trying to kill him by blowing up his car? There was so much more involved with this story that I couldn't figure out yet and it was pissing me off. I'd usually be farther along in a case by now, only I was left with more questions than I'd started with. What the hell was going on?

Dean took everything in stride, answering any questions he could while lying skillfully about the golf. I didn't usually make it a habit to lie, especially when it came to an investigation, but the cops would only get in the way of solving this case and we didn't have time for that. Someone was hot on our tails and they'd made sure we knew it.

Now it was time for some offense.

The valet felt so guilty over the whole exploding car thing it was easy to convince him to let me into the security room of the country club while Dean distracted the remaining police out front. The head security guard was more than willing to help me after seeing my detective license. It turned out he loved film noir and thought the whole thing was exciting. "What do you want to see?" he asked, a giddy smile on his face.

"I want to see the footage from the parking lot right before the explosion. The cameras must have caught it, right?"

The security guard nodded. "Should have." He pulled up the video and scrolled through the timeline. The parking lot was busy for most of the day and then the video went black.

"What just happened?"

The security guard furrowed his brow and pressed something on the keyboard. "I don't know." He slowed down the video and backed up to play it again.

About twenty minutes before the explosion the camera was fine. There was the Speedster all by itself at the end of the lot. Then blackness. "It looks like someone covered the lens." I leaned in to get a better look. "Probably spray paint, judging by the streakiness."

The security guard shook his head. "I don't understand. The valet must have seen someone doing that."

I thought back to how distracted our valet had been with his flirting and it made perfect sense. "Apparently not. Well thanks anyways."

So that was a bust. I should have known our stalker would have covered their tracks. They've been on top of everything.

I slipped back outside to Dean and shook my head.

"*Damn.*"

We'd played dumb and let the cops think that it was something faulty with the car, though any expert would be able to figure out the lie fairly quickly. By the time they let us go, it was dark and we were down one car. Dean called Felicity and she came to pick us up. She seemed more shaken by the whole thing than Dean himself. "So someone is following you two?" she asked as we got in. Crunching into a sitting position hurt everywhere, and a headache was forming behind my eyes.

"Looks like it. Someone is definitely watching us," Dean replied, which didn't seem like a terribly comforting thing to say, to me.

"This is actually good," I said.

She started the car and narrowed her eyes at me. "In what way is Dean's car getting bombed a good thing?" she asked, her tone sharp.

I shrugged. "It means we're pissing someone off, which means we're doing something correctly. We're on the right track."

"It was actually pretty exciting," Dean said with a smile, his eyes alight.

"Well I think you could do with less excitement, Dean," Felicity stressed. "This is like San Francisco all over again." She stopped abruptly after saying the words and glanced at me in the rearview mirror, then over at Dean.

In her haste she must have said something she wasn't meant to in front of me. Another one of Dean's many secrets.

Dean cleared his throat. "This is nothing like that, Felicity." He lowered his voice. "I promise."

She pressed her lips together and turned her attention to the road. The rest of the drive was silent until we pulled up to the office.

I said, "Thanks for the ride, Felicity," as I got out of the car. "Very sorry about the Speedster, Dean. Obviously I can't afford to replace it."

He waved his hand. "It wasn't your fault, detective. I knew there were going to be risks. Besides, if it wasn't for you we'd both be barbecue right now, so thank you."

"Yes, thank you, detective," Felicity added. "Dean is an impulsive knuckle-head, but I don't know what I'd do without him."

Dean squeezed her arm.

There was that twisting in my stomach again. Were they dating? They must be. They were too close for friends. They had this energy around them that I couldn't figure out. What was their deal?

I smiled, the movement painful to the cut above my eyebrow. "Happy to help."

"I'll see you bright and early, Noah?" Dean asked from the window.

"You still want to help me solve this case?" I would have figured this was the last straw. The act that finally scared him off. Interviewing people was one thing, getting followed and threatened with murder was another.

He pinched his brows. "Of course. What else would I be doing?"

I shrugged and crossed my arms. "I don't know, I thought maybe you'd be more concerned for your safety. It's not every day you get almost torn to pieces." I looked him in the eye. "Are you sure you feel safe by yourself? Whoever did this was threatening you just as much as they were threatening me."

He grinned. "Don't worry. Our apartment building is like Fort Knox. Nobody is getting past the front desk."

They lived in the same building? I hadn't realized, although it made sense. Did they live together, also? Rich people didn't need roommates, so if they *lived* together it could only mean one thing: my assumptions were correct, and they *were* dating. In whatever weird secretive way rich people dated.

"As long as you're sure. You can always sleep in the office," I offered.

He laughed. "I'm good, actually. See you in the morning, detective."

"Bye." I waved as they drove off.

When I got up to the apartment Captain greeted me with a sloppy kiss. "I missed you too, buddy. I threw my ruined suit jacket on the floor somewhere in my bedroom and changed into new clothes that weren't torn and covered in soot. I wanted a shower, however half my torso was covered in bandages, so I settled for washing my face in cold water and downing two pain pills.

Finding that I had no food to speak of in my fridge, I took Captain out for a walk that ended at Greta's diner. They didn't close until two in the morning and always had something hot—which was all I really wanted. I ate some hash browns and eggs, feeling more tense than usual. I found myself looking around, examining who was sitting close to me and looking out the window at the people walking by. Was I still being followed? Watched? Would I even notice if I was? I was usually the one *doing* the watching and it didn't feel great to have the roles reversed.

When I finished eating, I walked Captain back to the apartment. As soon as we entered the lobby Captain started barking. He never barked unless someone was around. I pulled out my taser that I'd grabbed earlier and walked up the stairs slowly, trying to hide myself from sight—though Captain kind of gave me away. Someone was standing at the top of the stairs outside my front door.

"Dean?"

He turned and smiled, first to me, then down at Captain. "Hey, boy, miss me already?" He knelt down to scratch behind the labradoodle's ear.

I slipped the taser back into my pocket. "What are you doing here? I thought you went home?"

"I did, then I remembered something important." He pulled the watch out of his pocket for me to see.

"Shit, right. I forgot about it myself with the cops and everything."

"Can I come in?" Dean asked, gesturing to the door behind him.

"Of course." I unlocked the door for him and we all shuffled inside, Captain nipping at Dean's heels.

"So, this watch is cheap," Dean said as he sat down at the small breakfast table.

I sat down on the other side, lucky I even had two chairs. "How do you figure?"

He set the watch on the table between us. "I can just tell. I've seen enough nice watches to know what they're supposed to look like and what a cheap imitation looks like. This is *definitely* a cheap imitation."

"*Hmm.*" I stared down at the watch. "I don't think many mobsters would be walking around with fake watches."

He grinned. "My thoughts exactly. And who do we know that wears cheap watches and cheap suits?"

I was following his train of thought. "Miguel Gomez."

He snapped his fingers. "Right. Everything about him is fake and cheap. It was one of the first things I noticed about him."

"And he doesn't have a solid alibi for the theft either. He was caught on the camera in the hallway."

Dean messed with the watch. "Look, the clasp on the wristband is broken. That's why it fell off. Cheap work."

He was right. So it *was* possible that the watch was a genuine clue. "Miguel is young and stupid, he has motive, and no alibi. It's not looking good for our social media star."

Dean beamed, leaning back in his chair. "No, it's not."

"We need to interview him first thing in the morning. I'll get Lexi to track him down. I don't think he's going to like us showing up and surprising him again."

"Probably not."

There was that telltale fluttering in my stomach and my chest was cramping in pain from the bruised ribs. I grimaced.

He pinched his brows and touched my hand across the table. "Are you okay?"

"I'm fine, just need a restful night's sleep and I'll be good as new in the morning."

He raised a skeptical eyebrow. "Okay, I'll leave you to get some rest, then."

"How'd you get here?" I asked. I hadn't noticed Felicity's car in the lot earlier.

"I got a cab."

I pushed myself up to stand. "I'll drive you home."

He shook his head. "That's not necessary, Noah. I can get another cab."

"*Or* you can save your money and accept a ride. Besides, you're safer with me. If someone actually is watching us it might be a good idea to stay together."

"Do you think they're going to blow up my cab?"

I shrugged. "No, probably not, though they might hire someone to pretend to be a cab driver."

He shuddered. "Okay, you win. You can drive me."

I locked up and we went downstairs to the back alley of the building. My Jeep was still there, right where I'd parked it. With great pain and discomfort I knelt down and examined the underside of the car with the flashlight on my phone.

"Any bombs?" Dean asked.

"No, it doesn't look like anyone has tried for a second round." If they had I would have caught it on the cameras, but now that I knew how tricky our criminal was I was taking *every* precaution.

"Great."

We got in the car and I drove Dean to his apartment, which as I'd suspected *was* in fact the same building where we'd picked up Felicity days earlier. I wanted to ask if they lived together, however it wasn't any of my business. Dean was a client, not a friend. He was paying me to solve this case. That's why I was doing all this—I needed the money. *Right?*

I parked the car along the front curb. The front desk was dark for the night. Nobody was around.

Dean was staring down at his lap, and then he shifted and looked me in the eye. "Thanks for everything, Noah. Not just the ride, but for saving my life earlier and doing everything you can to help me figure this out. It means a lot to me."

"I—you're welcome, Dean." I was lost for words. Sometimes clients were appreciative, however it was never personal. It was always business.

He went on, "I know this case has been more involved than either of us thought possible, and I know you could have dropped me if you wanted to. However, I'm glad that you didn't." He unbuckled his seat belt and I thought he was going to get out of the car, instead however, he leaned over and kissed me. I was so shocked I didn't react for a second.

He pulled back and read my face. "Oh, shit. *Sorry*, I wasn't thinking —"

I grabbed him by his lapels and pulled him back to me, closing the distance. His lips were soft and warm, and his hair smelled faintly of smoke. The storm in my stomach vanished, replaced by a calmness. I broke off and he slowly pulled away, his eyes never leaving mine.

It was hard to read his expression; after a few seconds he smiled. "I'll see you in the morning, Noah."

I waved lamely. "See you in the morning."

He gave me one long, final glance before slipping out of the Jeep, walking up the steps to his apartment building, and disappearing inside.

I started the car and pulled away into traffic.

Shit, I just kissed a client. That crossed all kinds of lines. What was I thinking? That was so unprofessional of me. It stirred up all kinds of emotions

I couldn't sort out. So Dean *wasn't* dating Felicity? Had I read them all wrong? I stopped at a red light. It was late at night and Downtown LA was busy as ever. Couples holding hands were walking down the sidewalk, and bars were lit up in bright colors from neon signs. A soft R&B beat was spilling out from one of the buildings.

I groaned, hitting my palm against the steering wheel. I couldn't do this. I needed to set things straight. As soon as the light turned green I pulled a u-turn and drove back up the street to his apartment. I didn't know how I was going to find him since I'd never asked for his actual apartment number. It must have been one of hundreds.

As I got closer, I saw someone running up to a cab that was waiting in front of the building. No, not just anyone. It was *Dean*. I'd know his silly striped suit anywhere.

"*What the hell?*" I whispered.

Why would he be getting into a cab after I had just dropped him off? Was he meeting someone? I thought he understood that he needed to hole up at home to stay safe. Why was he leaving late at night? The exact *opposite* of what I'd asked him to do? As I pulled up to the building the cab pulled away.

I decided rashly to follow the taxi. I needed to know what was so important that Dean couldn't wait until tomorrow to do it? If he'd needed something he could have asked me to drive him. Maybe he was feeling just as awkward about the kiss as I was and didn't want to talk.

I followed the cab a few cars lengths away like I'd taught Dean—turning when they turned, stopping when they stopped. They were heading east, back toward my side of town. Was he coming to see me? Again? That would be particularly awkward if I followed them to my own apartment. But no. They turned left where they should have turned right.

"Where the hell are you going, Dean?"

A couple blocks later the cab stopped again. This time, Dean got out. We were in a fairly nice neighborhood. It was a mix of modest middle class homes and cheap apartment buildings. Who could he be visiting that lived over here? And why?

I pulled over and parked half a block up so he wouldn't notice me. I followed him in my rearview mirror as he walked down the street and entered a mid-rise apartment building.

I got out of the car and jogged over. It wasn't anything like Dean's building. The front door didn't even have a security code to get in. I slipped inside and caught the back end of Dean on the floor above through the gaps of the stairwell. I followed as quickly and as quietly as I could, turning the corner on the second landing and peering around to see where he went next. The hallway was long and empty. It was all so very...average.

Dean stopped at a door near the end. I expected him to knock (as one does when they visit somebody), only he pulled out a key and unlocked the door himself. Why did he have a key to someone else's apartment? Was he housesitting for someone? Why not tell me that? None of this made sense. What the hell was he doing here? And what else was he keeping from me?

I crept down the hallway to the apartment. *Should I knock? Or should I just ignore this and bring it up later?*

No, I needed to understand what was *so* terribly important that Dean felt the need to put himself in a dangerous position. Was he followed here by whoever was watching us? I hadn't noticed anyone, but when dealing with a professional, anything was possible.

I waited a minute and let out a deep breath before knocking twice on the door. *He better have a good explanation for this.* I didn't care *how* much he was paying me.

FOURTEEN

When the door finally opened, Dean was standing there with a toothbrush in his mouth, his eyes wide.

"Uh, hi, Noah," he said around his full mouth.

"What the hell is going on here?" I gazed past him into the apartment. It seemed like a typical LA two-bedroom, decorated and filled with furniture and art.

"Um..." As he trailed off I realized he had nothing to say. I pushed past him into the room.

Sitting on the plush green couch in her pajamas was Felicity. She smiled awkwardly. "Hello?" She looked different without any makeup, but just as beautiful.

I spun around to face Dean who was spitting out his toothpaste into the kitchen sink to my left. "You have one minute to explain or I walk away." I was tired of the lying and the bullshit, the things that never quite added up correctly.

He wiped his chin and let out a shaky laugh. "It's uh, hard to explain."

I narrowed my eyes and crossed my arms. "Try me."

"Well you said we should take precautions so we—"

"Rented an apartment in the span of an hour?"

I took a better look around. Someone had clearly lived here for a while. The furniture was worn in, the walls were covered in art, and the kitchen sink was full of dishes.

"No, it's a friend's place. He's letting us stay here for the night because I explained the situation. You know, the whole *bombing* thing." He grinned as if I was supposed to find that funny.

I didn't laugh. I'd gotten to know Dean well enough over the last couple days to tell when he was putting on an act. He was being overly charming and casual on purpose, however I could see the fear behind his eyes.

I stood my ground. "Try again."

He faltered, taking a step back. "What—"

"I know that's not true, so try again."

He furrowed his brows and sputtered. "What do you mean *not true*? How dare you barge in here and call me a liar. What are you even doing here?" He'd dropped the charm and gone straight for confrontation.

"*What am I doing here?*" I asked harshly. What *was* I doing here? "I drove back to your apartment to talk and then I saw you getting into a *cab*. After I expressly forbid you from going anywhere for your own safety. You yourself told me how safe your high-rise was. Why would you come here?"

I looked between him and Felicity. Felicity, having not spent nearly as much time with me as Dean, appeared resigned—a rabbit caught in a trap. While Dean on the other hand, was still fighting tooth and nail.

He was wearing sweatpants and a t-shirt for once. It was strangely casual, normal. He put his hands on his hips. "What right do you have to follow me? It's no business of yours what I'm doing here or why."

"Fine...goodbye."

I turned to leave and Dean stepped out in front of me, his features cooling. "Wait! I'm sorry, that was harsh. I didn't mean that."

I crossed my arms again. "You're down to twenty seconds, Dean. What is going on here?"

"I—"

"And *don't* lie to me," I stressed. "I think you *owe* me that much."

He exhaled and glanced over at Felicity behind me.

"Your choice, darling," she said from across the room.

Dean turned back and caught my eye. "I'm not who I said I was."

"*Clearly,*" I mumbled.

He frowned. "Would you let me finish? You asked me to explain."

I gestured with my hand. "Please, go on."

"I'm not Mr. Williams' nephew."

The realization hit me like a brick wall. I hadn't even been thinking in that direction, though it suddenly made so much sense. I'd assumed Dean was lying about how much money he had, not about his connection to his so-called *uncle*.

I turned my focus back on him. "Then, who are you?"

He shrugged with a faint smile at the corner of his lips. "I'm...Dean, that's all."

I scoffed. "If that's not your uncle's house then how did you get access to it?"

He sighed, his shoulders dropping. "He hired me to be his security while he was on vacation. I was watching the house."

I was piecing it all together in my brain. "So you threw a party in a client's house?"

"Well, yes, I suppose so."

"So all this time you haven't been worried about Mr. Williams being angry because his nephew messed up, you've been worried that when he gets back and finds out what happened he's going to have you arrested?"

He nodded. "Correct."

Now it was making much more sense why Dean would invite a bunch of strangers to his *uncle's* house. He was a fraud. "Are you a con man?"

He rolled his eyes. "I wouldn't call it that. Con man is so low brow, what I do is more sophisticated."

"So you *are* a criminal."

"I take from corrupt people. Does that make me a criminal?" He furrowed his brow. "Do you think the world is going to weep because a racist multi-millionaire like *Daryl Hackney* is set back five percent? No."

I let out a bitter laugh through my nose. "So you're Robin Hood, then?"

He cocked his head to the side. "*Hmm*, I wouldn't say that, either."

I let out a deep breath. "What's to stop me from turning you in right now? From telling Warner that you're a fraud?"

He went still, his face pale. "I would hope you weren't that cruel, Noah. Yes, I lied to you, but the theft and the murder are very real and neither of which are my fault."

I hadn't been thinking about that either until he'd said it. Could Dean be involved with the theft? The murder? What did I *truly* know about him? What was real and what was simply an act? "Who are you?" I asked again, quieter this time.

He shrugged and took a step forward. "I'm Dean Prescott. I enjoy fine dining, walks on the beach, luxury suits, and driving my Speedster around the city with my friends. Or I *did* enjoy driving my Speedster, may she rest in peace."

"This is no time for jokes, Dean," I spat out. "I could have you arrested with *one* phone call."

"Please don't." His dark eyes searched mine. "I've worked hard to build this life. *Extremely* hard."

I scoffed. "Is my check going to bounce when I cash it?"

He frowned. "Of course not. I would never do that."

"And where did the money come from?"

He faltered.

"That's what I thought." I turned to step past him. "I'll work to finish this case, but you will have *no more* involvement. I'll decide at the end whether to turn you two in or not. Hand me the watch."

He ran to the other room and came back with the timepiece. "*Noah.*"

I whipped around. "That's Detective Sun to you, Mr. Prescott. I'll contact you in a couple days." I took the watch and opened the door.

"I—"

"*What?*"

He put his hands in his pockets. "I'm sorry, detective. I wasn't trying to stir up trouble for you."

"Too late." I closed the door with more force than necessary and stalked down the stairs and out the front door.

How could he think that I wouldn't figure him out eventually? I'd known that he was hiding something from me from the start. *Stupid.* I should have spotted it sooner. *That's* why he couldn't contact his uncle. He'd probably found a way to make that impossible, hedging off the inevitable. He'd lied to *me*, but also to the *police*. And now I was complicit if I didn't turn them in.

I drove home in anger, speeding more than I should have and running at least one red light. When I got to the apartment I pulled a beer out of the fridge and chugged it down, before slamming it on the table. Captain barked at the noise and came over to investigate. His presence calmed me down slightly. I rubbed behind his ears and sipped on the rest of the bottle, stewing.

This was all such a mess. I couldn't connect the lying con man persona with the Dean who'd been driving me around for days. The Dean who laughed at everything and always made the hard choices. He'd been in my apartment, worn my clothes...kissed me. Was that all a part of the act? To get me to help him stay out of jail? To manipulate me?

It had to be.

I'd caught him and now it was over. However, I couldn't abandon the case altogether. There was still a theft and a murder to solve. Whether Dean committed them I wasn't certain. Anything was possible now. How many other lies had he told? And why had it taken so long for me to figure it out? I'd been distracted. I'd gotten soft. I'd let Dean's charms affect me. I'd known something was wrong from the start, and I'd ignored it. Ignored my better judgment. Well no more. I was back at one hundred percent and I was going to solve this case no matter what happened. Even if I had to arrest Dean myself.

I grabbed my laptop from the office and started researching anything I could find on Dean Prescott—if that was even his real name. What came up was, surprise, surprise, very little. He'd probably worked hard to keep himself off the internet. What was available through public records and detective search engines was a picture of an average upper-class man. No arrests, just a slew of parking tickets (of course). No known family—no siblings, no cousins even. Were his parents even dead? That whole sob story he'd told me at the police station, had it all been a lie? I didn't see any death certificates for them. Somehow he'd scraped everyone associated with him from the internet. I wondered how much that cost.

He had no social media that I could find. He was unmarried, had never owned property, and had no important financial or legal filings. Which was highly suspicious considering he was supposedly a *businessman*. How had he pulled that off? More back-door trickery, no doubt. More greased palms.

On paper there was nothing interesting about Dean Prescott. Nothing at all. He'd made sure of it.

I closed my laptop and got another beer from the fridge. This was why I worked better alone. I didn't need anyone. Not Malcolm, and certainly not Dean.

Tomorrow I would end this case. The sooner I solved it, the sooner I'd have Dean out of my life. *Forever*.

FIFTEEN

Captain left a slobbery kiss on my cheek, his face looming above mine. "Okay, I'm up. *Stop.*" I gently pushed him aside and sat up in bed. I had a lot to sort out today.

I found two new texts on my phone and deleted both without reading them. Ignoring Dean was going to be no challenge. I was used to working alone. It's what I was comfortable with. I didn't need someone hanging on my sleeve, dragging me back. Maybe this case would have been solved already if Dean hadn't been slowing me down at every turn with his annoying antics and displays of drama.

I threw off my covers and got dressed in a rush. I took Captain out for a short walk and then started my day. I downed a whole mug of black coffee and ran out the door. I was wary of the fact that someone could still be watching me, watching Dean, so I took the Jeep for a ride around the block, turning one way and then the other in a figure-eight, until finally turning toward the North-East side of LA. If someone *was* following me they'd have a fun time catching up now.

I had a few choice words for Miguel. I was done playing Mr. Nice Guy. When I knocked on his front door his mother answered instead. "Yes?" She was wearing casual clothes—a blouse and jeans—but had on a bright purple lipstick that seemed out of place.

"Is Miguel home?" I asked, getting straight to the point.

She narrowed her eyes, surveying me. "Why do you want to know?"

I pulled out my detective's license. "I need to speak with him in regards to a murder." Why not be blunt? I didn't have time left for subtlety.

She took a step back, her hand on her chest. "*What?*"

"He didn't tell you?"

She shook her head, her eyes wide. "My son would never be involved in a—in a murder."

"That's for *me* to decide. Do you know where he is?"

Her features relaxed and she shrugged. "No idea."

221

She was lying, though there was no sense in pointing that out. Intimidating a woman wasn't my style, even if I *was* pissed as all hell. "Fine. I'll find out some other way."

I turned to leave and she shut the door behind me. This wasn't going at all how I wanted. I texted Lexi and then checked the time. She was at school. I wasn't *technically* supposed to be asking her for favors when she was studying. What kind of uncle was I if I did? However, today was an exception. The faster I closed this case, the faster I could get Dean and his well-tailored suits out of my hair for good.

N: Can you help me find out where Miguel Gomez is today? He's not at home.

She responded almost immediately.

L: Give me two seconds.

After a minute or two she called. "Let me look real quick." Rushing water almost drowned out her voice.

"Where are you?"

She laughed through her nose. "I had to fake a period crisis to use the restroom. Mr. Hardy is an ass, but he's scared of girls, so *one* mention of anything period related and he folds."

I shook my head. "I'm sorry to ask you for a favor when you're at school."

She blew out a quick breath. "You're saving me from boredom, really, Uncle Noah. I should be *thanking* you."

I laughed for the first time that day. "Your intelligence is definitely wasted on that expensive private school your parents send you to."

"Tell me about it." A few seconds passed in silence. "I got him."

"Really?"

"Uh-huh. He posted on his story an hour ago that he's showing a house in North Hollywood today. I found the address on his website." She named off the address. "I'll text it to you too."

"Thanks, kid." I smiled. "What would I do without you?"

She laughed. "You'd figure it out eventually. And I'm not a kid anymore, Uncle Noah."

I sighed. "I know, it's scary how fast you're growing up. Soon you'll be in college and I'll just be some old fart you used to help out sometimes."

She giggled. "You're not old. You're...experienced."

"Another word for old, but thanks. I appreciate it. Go back to class.

She groaned. "Do I have to?"

"Yes, you do."

"Okay. Bye."

"Bye." I hung up the phone and found the address in her text. I'd thought about telling her how Dean was a liar, that he'd scammed us, only she didn't need to know. She was busy being a teenager, she didn't need my problems. Who *could* I tell? I had a small, dwindling number of friends that spoke to me. Most of which had chosen Malcolm in the breakup. My best friend couldn't be my sixteen-year-old niece. That was pathetic and unhealthy.

Dammit Dean. I tensed my hands into fists and then restarted the car. I needed to forget about him. He *wasn't* a friend. He wasn't *anything* anymore. He was a liar, and I was a detective—someone who caught liars for a living.

I punched the address into my phone and drove off towards Hollywood. Today I had one goal and Dean wasn't a part of that.

* * *

I rolled up to the curb in front of the house and parked. There were a couple cars already in the driveway—people who had arrived for the showing. I wondered which car Miguel was renting, or whatever he was doing, to fake his status. The house was gargantuan and ugly as hell, all white and cement. It was the exact opposite of homey—the LA fantasy.

I marched up the drive and through the open front door. A blonde woman with a high ponytail and heels much too tall to walk in handed me a flier as I entered. She looked me up and down, obviously noticing from my attire that I wasn't going to be buying the house. "Just looking around?" she asked politely.

What would Dean do? I hated that the thought entered my brain, but he *would* know what to do, how to act. I pulled my shoulders back and stood up as straight as possible. "My usual agent has been finding absolute crap in this neighborhood and if I have to be any farther away from the 405 I'm going to kill myself," I said as monotone and prick-ish as possible. "What's the asking price?"

It seemed to do the trick. The blonde changed her demeanor immediately. "Of course, sir. They're asking three point six with a free inspection and no closing costs."

"*Hmm*, acceptable. I'm going to look around."

She smiled. "Of course, if you have any questions, Miguel, the lead agent, is walking around upstairs."

I didn't spare her a second glance, "Thanks," before finding the stairs and taking them two at a time. I found Miguel and an older White couple walking around in the main bedroom which had a wall of windows and a terrace looking out over the city. It was a stunning view. A view I'd likely never be able to afford.

Miguel faltered when he spotted me and then smiled even harder. "Come on in, look around. I'll be here if you have any questions."

As soon as the couple left to look at the adjoining bathroom I cornered Miguel. His smile dropped. "What do you want now?"

"I have some unanswered questions, Miguel. It's time for you to answer them."

He narrowed his eyes and crossed his arms. "What?"

I pulled out the watch from my coat pocket and held it in front of his face. "Does this look familiar?"

He examined it for a second, his eyes widening. "Where'd you get my watch? Did you take that from my house? What the hell?"

I laughed through my nose. "Funnily enough, I found it next to the car that almost exploded with me in it. Care to comment on that, Miguel?"

I hadn't thought it possible, however, his eyes got even wider, and his jaw ground nervously. "*What?* What the hell are you saying, man? I don't know anything about no exploding car. Who the hell do you think I am?"

I leaned in closer. "A liar at minimum. The rest I'm just starting to figure out."

"Man, get the hell out of here," he spit. "I don't have to talk to you."

The older couple left the bathroom and Miguel smiled carefree as they walked down the stairs. If they'd heard us arguing they didn't show it.

"*Hmm*, that's true, I suppose. I guess I'll tell the cops to go interview you and your mom. I'm sure she'd be more than happy to cooperate when it comes to a murder investigation."

"Murder?" He took a step back and hit the wall. "What the hell are you on about? Before, you said something was *stolen*."

I pinched my brows in faux confusion. "Did I not mention the murder? The man stabbed to death in the same house where you partied the night before?" I held up the watch again. "And now I find a watch of yours at *another* crime scene. Things are not looking good for you, Miguel."

His breathing increased speed. "I didn't have anything to do with any of that. This is harassment."

"Right, well as far as I know you don't have an alibi for any of these crimes, so what's it going to be? Where were you at eight o'clock on Saturday morning? Huh? Because your *neighbor* didn't corroborate anything you told us." I hadn't actually checked with the neighbor, however the bluff worked perfectly.

He looked down at the floor. "I was—I was at my sister's school."

"At your sister's school?" I scoffed. "On a Saturday?"

"They were doing a...fall performance," he got out through gritted teeth.

"Who was she playing?" I asked, just for the fun of it.

"She was an apple, man. I filmed the whole thing, so don't give me any more shit."

I shrugged. "Okay, so you're not a killer. What about the theft during the party?"

He crossed his arms, trying to look tough. "I already told you I didn't take anything."

"And yet you were caught on camera in the hallway right when it was stolen, so you're going to have to do better than that, Miguel."

He put his hands out. "Give me some freaking space to breath, man."

I took a small step back. "Fine, you think for a moment. But don't take too long."

He stared down at the hardwood floors, his jaw grinding and popping. "When was it exactly? The camera thing?"

"12:13."

"Oh shit, wait." He fumbled for his phone before pulling it out of his back pocket. "I think..." He opened something on his phone and started messing with it.

"You think *what*?" I was getting impatient. I didn't have time to be jerked around.

He looked up, his golden eyes searing into me. "I think I was live at the time."

"Live?"

"On *social media*," he replied like *I* was the biggest idiot in the room.

Yeah, that role was already taken, pal.

"It's still there in my archive." He pulled up a video and showed me his phone. In the corner it was timestamped. Saturday, 12:10.

I grabbed the phone and dragged the video bar forward. Miguel was hanging out in the hall for a bit and then he was showing off the lounge with all the guests. Mrs. Wong scowled at him. Dean noticed the camera and waved with a charming smile. Nothing amiss.

So there was no possible way that Miguel could have stolen the statue at 12:13 when he was walking toward the lounge at that time with thousands of people watching him. Unless this was all an elaborate game, Miguel was cleared, for both the theft *and* the murder.

"If that's true, how do you explain your watch at the scene of a crime?"

He shook his head. "I don't know. It's not like my house is Fort Knox or something—my ma would let anyone in. Someone is *obviously* framing me, man. Do I look like a thief to you?"

I sighed, my shoulders deflating. "I'm going to choose not to answer that question. If I find out that anything you've told me is a lie in any way, I'll be back Mr. Gomez, and you'll be screwed."

He shook his head again. "I didn't do shit. Why would I? I'm doing well for myself." He gestured around the room as if that was proof.

"You live in the suburbs with your mom and little sister," I reminded him.

He narrowed his eyes. "Yeah, and I paid off my ma's mortgage, *dumbass*. Her car too."

Huh. "Aw, family values. That *almost* makes me like you, Miguel."

He blew out a breath through his teeth. "Whatever."

I gave him a final look over before saying, "Don't leave town, Miguel. I'll know if you do."

He rolled his eyes.

"Have fun with the open house. I think three point six is a little steep for this area. You'll probably still sell, though."

He scoffed as I left the room. When I passed the first woman downstairs I frowned and said in a haughty voice, "Too many windows, and yet, not enough light."

She smiled, though her brows were furrowed. "*Oh*, okay."

"Goodbye." I left and got back in the car.

So, Miguel was out. He would have been the perfect suspect. This could only mean one thing. Someone had planted the watch for us to find. They were playing games, cat and mouse. Had the bomb truly been meant to kill us or only to scare us? There were so many layers to this circus show. The suspects were dwindling quickly and there were only so many without solid alibis remaining. I needed to reinterview all our previous suspects now that we knew the exact time the statue was stolen.

Back on the road, my phone started to buzz. I glanced down. Dean's number was flashing across the screen. What did *he* want? Hadn't I made it clear that I wanted nothing to do with him and that I'd solve the case on my own? Had he decided to beg for my forgiveness?

I reluctantly picked up the call, figuring it might be something about the investigation. "*What?*" I said as bored as I could muster.

"Hey, Noah."

"*What?*" I repeated.

"So...I'm in jail."

SIXTEEN

"You're what?" I pulled over to the side of the road and gave the call my full attention. "What do you mean you're in jail?"

"They arrested me about an hour ago."

I scoffed. "For what?" Had Dean's conning finally caught up to him? But then why hadn't Warner called me?

He hesitated. "They're saying that I staged my car exploding. Someone called in a tip that I faked the whole thing."

"Faked it?" That made even less sense. "For what reason?"

"For attention, I guess. They arrested me for public endangerment, unlawful use of explosives, and damage to private property."

My chest tightened. "That's bullshit, they have no evidence. Who arrested you?"

"Who do you think?"

"Warner?" I didn't think he would stoop so low. Or be so dumb. "Who sent in the tip?"

He scoffed, barely hiding the bitterness in his voice. "It was *anonymous.*"

"So it could be anyone, then. Probably our killer trying to throw suspicion off of themselves. What reason did they give for arresting you?"

He laughed through his nose. "Whoever called in told them I had a history of faking spectacle for police attention."

"Meaning?"

He was silent on the other end of the line.

"*Meaning?*" I asked again.

"I *might* have staged a certain situation one time and then anonymously called the police to make the situation seem more serious than it was to scare one of my marks, and the police *might* have learned my real name from that instance. It was a super long time ago, more than ten years. I was a teenager. Those records are supposed to be sealed."

Great.

"You gotta get me out of here, Noah."

My first instinct was to agree with him, however, then I thought it through for a second. If someone *was* trying to kill Dean and get him out of the way, the police station *would* be the safest place for him. They were good for that much at least. And if he was locked up he wouldn't get in the way of my investigation and I could solve it that much faster knowing he was safe.

I cleared my throat and said dryly, "I'm a little busy, Dean."

"Yeah and I'm a little busy sitting in jail, Noah! You know I didn't do this, come get me out. *Please*. You can't still be *that* mad at me."

I was still *that* mad at him, though I was equally mad at the injustice of the police arresting someone without evidence of a crime. "I'm so close to solving this case. Once I solve it you'll be out quickly. Just hang tight."

"That's not what I meant. I don't want to be stuck in here!"

"Gotta go," I said quickly.

"*Noah*."

"Sorry, but you'll be fine." I hung up the phone and set it down. That was a *little bit* satisfying, a little bit. And besides, he'd be out by the end of the day if my logic was correct. The police didn't have anything to hold him on other than the bogus tip and a ten-year-old juvie misdemeanor.

Maybe a taste of jail was exactly what Dean needed in order to straighten his life out—like a night in the drunk tank. He'd be fine. I was sure he'd put himself in worse situations, knowing his line of work. The thought of him in his suit sitting next to a big drunk guy slobbering all over the place brought a smile to my face. Yes, *I think he'll be just fine.*

* * *

I pulled back onto the road with the full intention of driving straight to Rose Catering Company, when my phone started buzzing again. "Dammit, Dean, I said no." I looked down again at the caller ID. It wasn't Dean. Worse. It was my mother.

I could ignore the call, however I'd already put her off a couple days ago by not accepting her dinner invitation. If I ignored her again she'd track me down by *any* means necessary.

I picked up the call and put it on speaker. "Hi, Mom."

"Hi? That's all I get? You haven't spoken to me in over a week and all I get is a *hi*?"

I rolled my eyes and let out a silent sigh. "How are you? How's Dad? How's the weather down south?" My parents lived on the edge of LA closest to Orange County and we always joked about how much hotter it was *down south*.

She hummed. "Your father is fine and the weather is nice. Not too hot yet this spring, my roses are loving it. Now what's this about you not coming to dinner tonight because of some case?"

I knew she'd find a way to bring it up again. "Yeah, I got a big client right now. I've been working on it all week. I can't come to dinner, Mom."

She huffed. "You still have to eat, don't you, Noah? Are you not eating?" Concern edged her voice. "Tell me you're eating, Noah."

"I'm eating, Mom."

Her tone brightened. "Good, then you can make it to dinner. Be here in an hour."

"*Mom.*"

"Don't, *Mom*, me. You can cut out an hour or two to spend time with your family. Your brother wants to talk to you about Lexi, anyway. He thinks she's spending too much time over at your office, and well...I'll let him speak for himself."

That would be a change.

I glanced at my watch. It was already past noon. If I drove all the way to this dinner and back I wouldn't have time to interview Max before the kitchen closed. On the other hand, if he *was* on to me like I suspected he might be, ignoring him for a few hours could throw him off. It *could* make him relax, make a mistake.

"Okay, I'll be there."

"Great, bring wine, that kind that Malcolm always brought. What was it called?"

"Will do, bye, Mom."

She might have had other things to say, but I ended the call, punching the phone with my thumb. My parents even preferred Malcolm's *wine* choices.

I stopped at the liquor store and texted Lexi that I'd be coming over soon.

L: Perfect, we can strategize.

Leave it to Lexi to turn an awkward family dinner into a business opportunity. I still hadn't told her what I'd learned about Dean. I didn't know if I should or not. She'd been right from the start. Dean was slimy and he'd hidden things from us. I shouldn't have taken the case—as desperate as I was. The thought made me laugh as I bought the annoyingly expensive wine with what was, no doubt, money from Dean's deposit. His *dirty* money. My smile soured.

The drive to my parents' house was annoying and I got stuck in traffic for at least half an hour. So I was worked up by the time I pulled into their driveway. My parents' house was nice, though not over the top. Dad was an accountant and Mom had been a nurse before she retired early when she unexpectedly fell pregnant with me, ten years after my brother.

I entered the house without knocking, taking my boots off at the door. My parents were strictly *no* shoes. I shoved my feet into my old house slippers that still waited in the cubby by the entrance. My dad's family came from Korea and he still followed some of their traditions from his upbringing.

The house was quiet except for the low murmur of the TV in the other room. I followed the sound and found my dad sitting on the couch watching the news at a low volume. The news upset my mother, so he always watched it when she wasn't around. "Hey, Dad." I held up the wine bottle. "Brought some wine."

He gazed up at me. "Oh, good. Your mom said you were coming." He raised an eyebrow. "How's business?"

I forced a smile. "Good. I'm working a case right now."

He nodded and turned back to the TV. "Good, good."

And that was the end of the conversation. I walked through the living room to the kitchen and set the bottle of wine on the bar-height counter. Mom was standing by the stove opening tinfoil-covered takeout containers.

"Hey, Mom."

She turned and smiled, her crimson lipstick parting against white teeth. "Noah, you made it," she said as if I had an option of *not* coming. She was wearing a long red dress and had her short blonde hair in loose curls. She always dressed for family dinner and disapproved when *I* didn't. She looked me up and down, at the khakis and leather jacket. "Too bad you couldn't stop at home before coming here."

"I was already halfway across town," I explained, and she smiled, like she accepted my excuse. *She didn't.*

"That's fine. You can wear one of your dad's old suit jackets."

"Or I could wear what I'm wearing right now, Mom."

She smiled, a challenge behind her eyes. "Fine. Dinner will be ready in twenty minutes."

I jerked my chin at the aluminum takeout containers. "Kim's?"

She nodded. Kim's was our favorite Korean restaurant that did family-sized takeout. Mom wasn't much of a cook, to Dad's disappointment, however neither was he. Growing up we'd had a Korean nanny who cooked and taught us little bits of Korean here and there. Dad had made sure of it, or more likely, my grandparents had made sure of it. They didn't want us to lose our cultural heritage even though my dad had married a White woman.

"I'm gonna go see Lexi."

She smiled. "Okay. Your brother and Vivian should be here soon."

I'd arrived before my brother, that should win me some brownie points. On the other hand, Mark didn't need brownie points. He always got the whole pan of brownies no matter what. That's what happened when you were a doctor with a successful wife and prodigy child compared to a college dropout private detective with no savings and no clients.

I jogged up the stairs to the computer room/library where Lexi spent all her time when she was at her grandparents' house. She was so independent it didn't surprise me at all that she'd Ubered her way here before her parents.

I opened the door and found Lexi reading something on her tablet, hanging off the side of the sofa. "Hey."

She glanced up and dropped her reading. "You came."

I shrugged. She knew I didn't have a choice.

She nodded. "Right. So how about the case? Did you and Dean come up with anything after talking to Hackney? You went silent after that."

I cringed, remembering I hadn't told her about the exploding Speedster yet, either. It had been a *very* long couple of days. "So about that." I filled her in on the exploding car, keeping all the harrowing details to myself and making it seem *way* less dangerous than it actually was.

Her eyes went wide. "Someone tried to kill you?"

I put my finger to my lips and she quieted down. "Uh, kind of."

"What kinda answer is that?" she whispered loudly. "It's a yes or no question!"

I sat down on the sofa beside her. "Then yes, but we're both fine."

She raised an eyebrow. "So you don't have *any* injuries at all?"

"I'm sorry, I should have told you. But I'm okay. See?" I shook out my arms and my legs and *almost* didn't wince from the pain.

She clearly didn't buy what I was selling. "I can see that cut above your eye." She narrowed her gaze, squinting at my forehead.

I blew out a breath. "Superficial." I decided to change the subject. "Also, Dean is sort of in jail right now because the police think he staged the whole thing, though that's a different situation entirely."

Her mouth dropped open. "*What?*"

I hesitated, and then told her everything that had happened last night, including finding out Dean was a lying liar con artist who'd scammed us. How I'd followed him home to his secret second apartment and found out he wasn't really a millionaire playboy.

She was less mad than I thought she'd be. She furrowed her brow. "I'm sorry, Uncle Noah."

"*Sorry?*" Why was *she* sorry? Lexi usually sniffed out liars. She hated when people were dishonest with her.

She shrugged one shoulder. "I know you liked him."

I scoffed. "I didn't *like* him. He was annoying and got in the way of the investigation. I'm glad he's safely in a jail cell right now. It leaves me time to finish this case without him interfering. So why should you be sorry?"

She hesitated. "Because he...made you smile."

I frowned. "He *what*?"

"He made you smile; he made you laugh. You've been all doom and gloom ever since Malcolm left and these past few days I've finally seen the old you reappear."

The back of my neck flushed. I knew Lexi was observant, only I hadn't realized she'd been directing her observations *at me*.

"What are you saying, Lexi? He's a con artist."

She waved her hands. "I know. That doesn't mean that everything about him was fake, though."

I begged to differ. "Um, that's *exactly* what it means. It's in the name. He played me to gain my confidence."

"His payment went through, though," she said as if it was some consolation.

"Yeah, and he most likely *stole* that money. We've been paid with stolen funds. That makes us complicit."

She rolled her eyes. "Calm down, Uncle Noah. You know that's not true."

"Maybe not, but when the police find out what he's done they're going to audit all of his payments. We can't accept his money. The only reason I'm continuing the case in the first place is because someone is dead and I can't let the police mess this one up, can I?"

She smiled. "Right, that's the *only* reason. It's not because you want to help Dean or that you like his company?"

"*Like* his company? He's annoying and over the top. He's always getting in my way and saying the wrong thing. Always messing things up."

She smiled. "And yet you still like him. I can tell."

I scoffed. There was *no way* I was telling Lexi about the kiss. That stayed between the two of us, and I was trying hard to pretend like it didn't happen. It made everything worse. How stupid was I to think Dean had liked me for me? That he was genuinely interested in helping to solve the case? It had all been a game. One big, complicated game.

"He's safest in jail," I reiterated. "As soon as I solve this case he'll get out and we'll part ways. It's what's best for everyone."

"Are you going to turn him in?" she asked with a raised eyebrow.

"*Hmm*, I haven't decided yet." I'd been rolling the idea around in my brain all morning.

She pouted. "You can't, Uncle Noah."

"What?" I caught her gaze. "Why not? He *lied* to me. Not to mention the thievery."

"What thievery?"

"Well that's not his uncle's house, obviously. He's squatting in someone else's mansion. That's a major crime. And now there's a big blood stain in the front entry. The cleaning bill alone is worth jail time."

She rolled her eyes again. "Oh my God, be reasonable, Uncle Noah."

I crossed my arms. "I *am* being reasonable, Lexi. This is just how it's going to be."

She stared me down, and when she realized I wasn't budging, she sighed. "Fine. But maybe you'll change your mind at the end of all of this."

I shrugged as if there was little chance.

"Lexi?" a voice called from downstairs.

"Your parents are here," I said, stating the obvious.

"Yippee. Let's go do this thing, I guess."

I mirrored her enthusiasm as I followed her downstairs to the living room. Mark and Vivian were dressed for dinner. Of course they were. Mark spotted me coming down the stairs and nodded in his usual manner.

"Hi, Mark."

Lexi hugged her dad and kissed her mom on the cheek. Mark checked his watch. "How'd you get here so fast after school?"

Lexi smiled. "School was cut early because of a test."

I noticed the lie immediately, yet Mark just nodded. "Okay, you should have at least texted us. Let's go eat."

I greeted Vivian with a smile and we followed the group into the dining room that lay in an open space between the living room and the kitchen. My mom had arranged most of the food on the table and my dad had turned off the news. He was messing with a corkscrew and the bottle of wine I'd brought. Mark held up a second bottle. "I brought a spare, just in case."

Of course he did.

I sat near the end closest to my mother at the head of the table, and Lexi sat across from me. Mark and Vivian sat across from each other with my dad at the other end of the table. I immediately picked up a dish of japchae and began serving out a portion before passing it along to Mark. I knew that if I was *eating* I didn't have to be *talking* and that everyone else would have a lot to say regardless.

"So," Mom started. "I hear from your parents that your grade has been dropping in Physics, Lexi. How come?"

Of course *this* would be the first topic of discussion. Lexi was used to the scrutiny, as was I, yet she still flushed at the accusatory tone. "Um, it was only midterms, the grades don't count until June."

Mark shook his head imperceptibly. "That doesn't change the fact that you got a C on a big test, sweetie. That tutor we hired was supposed to be helping you. Is he?"

Lexi stared at me across the table with pleading eyes.

Dang, why did I love that kid so much. I cleared my throat. "So my latest case is a murder. Pretty high profile," I added—as if murder wasn't enough to make my mother gasp beside me.

"Noah, I've told you not to mention things like that at the dinner table!" She leaned in closer to me. "Lexi is impressionable and some of your cases are so...awful," she stage whispered.

Lexi, of course, heard everything she said and rolled her eyes out of sight from her grandmother.

"I was just trying to make conversation." I smiled and grabbed the next side dish—fermented spring onions in a spicy gochujang sauce.

"Let's not talk about that particular, disturbing topic," Mom added.

My career? My whole life?

"You don't talk about the details of your cases with our daughter, I hope?" Mark asked to my left.

I shook my head. "Of course not. She helps organize my files and sort my payments for me. Nothing graphic."

"We wanted to talk you about this later, but it seems now is appropriate." Mark continued. "With Lex's declining grades Vivian and I think it would be best if Lexi took a break from working for you."

Lexi let out a sharp breath across from us. "What? Dad, you can't be serious."

He held up his hand, a warning. "Just until your grades improve, then we can renegotiate. Working for your uncle is a *privilege*, you have to earn it."

I clenched my fist underneath the table. Lexi was Mark's kid. I had no right to doubt his parenting skills since I had no kids of my own, but *man* I wanted to slap him upside the head.

Lexi immediately deflated across the table. She knew that arguing with her dad wouldn't get her anywhere. Once he made a decision, it was final.

I smiled to break the tension. "Okay, that's fine." I focused on Lexi, who I could tell was not feeling *fine*. "I'll give you your paycheck on Friday and then you can focus on your studies until you get that physics grade back up. Knowing you, I bet you can fix it quickly."

She gave me a small half-smile and turned her attention back down to her plate.

Mark nodded and hummed in agreement. I could tell he was satisfied I hadn't fought him on the decision like I normally would.

Vivian was quiet, as usual. She went with whatever choice Mark made—at least when they were in public.

My dad grunted at the end of the table. "Good. When I was a teenager my parents had the same idea. I got to work at the family restaurant to earn some money if I kept all A's. Then that money was put into my college fund. It got me through all four years of UCLA."

I wanted to remind my dad that UCLA was probably dirt cheap in the eighties compared to today's prices, but I stopped myself. It wouldn't do any good.

Mom set down her chopsticks and clapped her hands. "Let's have some nice conversation. Mark, weren't you telling me about the sweetest little girl who had a bee sting at your practice this week?"

He smiled and went into the story. I drowned it out—as nice as a cute kid medical miracle was. I could tell Lexi was doing the same. She looked up at me, her features miserable and I winked. She smiled.

* * *

At the end of dinner Dad lured Mark into having a scotch, Mom and Vivian talked quietly in the kitchen, and I followed Lexi up to the library. We were playing cards, however I could tell that Lexi's heart wasn't in the game. I beat her three times in a row and she usually *never* let me win.

"You know I'm not actually going to bar you from the office, right?"

She looked up, her eyes alight. "But you said—"

246

I rolled my eyes. "I know what I said, Lex. I also know you're smart as a whip and shouldn't be hindered by a silly physics grade. You're going to ace that final, right? I see you studying all the time."

She nodded. "Yeah."

I shrugged. "Then I'm not worried. Why should I be? I trust you."

Her lips tugged into a small smile. "So you're not kicking me off the case?"

"Of course not, we're almost at the end. I've narrowed it down to one, maybe two suspects, Dean is safe in jail, and the police are clueless as all hell. I still have a couple tricks up my sleeve for tomorrow."

"Can I come with?" Lexi asked with a bright, hopeful tone.

I shook my head and gathered up the cards on the table. "No, not on your life. What would your parents do to me if I let you get hurt?"

She pouted and crossed her arms. "Who says I would get hurt? I was the best in gym class during our self-defense course. I could kick some bad guy ass."

I cracked a grin and chuckled. "I'm sure you could Lexi, however that would be incredibly irresponsible to even put you in a position where you would *need* to kick some ass, so unfortunately the answer is still no."

She groaned. "Fine. Call me as soon as you make the arrest, though."

I winked. "Will do. Make sure to get your homework done tonight, and if you could, please take Captain out after school. I don't know when I'll be back."

She rolled her eyes. "How can I have one of the coolest part-time jobs in the world and still get stuck doing homework?"

I shrugged. "Your life just sucks, I guess."

She groaned again.

"If you stick around tomorrow I'll bring back ice cream to celebrate, how about that?"

"Rocky Road?" she asked hopefully.

I scrunched up my features. "Of course. Who do you take me for? An amateur?"

She giggled and then stood to hug me goodbye. "Fine, go catch the bad guy for me, Uncle Noah."

I smiled. "Promise."

Tomorrow I'd end this thing once and for all.

SEVENTEEN

There was only one person left on the suspect list who had the opportunity, the motive, and who matched all the evidence. Max Spade. Sure, he was a drunk, but that was easy to fake. His only alibi was catching the servers in the closet, which didn't account for all the time he was alone in the kitchen by himself. Plus, everyone would have overlooked him as the help. *We* overlooked him, thinking he was only a drunk with no motive. Even on Saturday, his alibi for the murder was shaky at best. He could have been gone for an hour and the two lovebirds wouldn't have noticed at all.

He was disregarded by others, he was good with knives, and he had lots of debt as I'd discovered during a frantic research session yesterday after I got home from my parents' house—so he was a prime choice for Teddy Lazzo to get his claws into. Plus, he had opportunity. He was in the right place at the right time. Everything fit.

I'd walked Captain earlier in the morning and left him a nice treat to occupy him until Lexi came by after school. Though I was imagining this would end quickly now that I was so close. It could all tumble down like dominoes, one detail after the other.

I'd driven to the catering kitchen first since I figured that was where Max would most likely be. The sad, beige building hadn't changed since Saturday.

I went around to the back and the emergency exit door was still propped open by a milk crate. I breathed out a sigh of relief. I wanted the element of surprise this time. If Max *was* who had been following us and planting evidence, then he knew I was coming for him. I didn't need to give him any more leverage against me.

I slipped past the door, leaving the crate where it was, trying to be as quiet as possible. The kitchen itself was silent—no chopping, no steaming, no sizzling. The lights were off, leaving the space dim, with the only light coming in from the hallway. Was nobody home? Then why was the door still open? Surely he wasn't *that* stupid.

I edged around the counter to the other side of the professional, galley-style kitchen. My foot hit something solid—a metal bowl. Pots and pans were strewn across the floor, onions, carrots, and broken jars of spices. Signs of a struggle. I paused and pulled out Tasha the taser to arm it before shaking out my free hand. Was someone still here? Hiding in the shadows? It was dead quiet. Too quiet.

I maneuvered around the crap on the ground to the other side of the kitchen near the industrial gas range. A figure lay slumped over on the floor. "Shit." I quickened my pace while remaining silent. Whoever did this could still be hanging around. Or maybe not if they left the back door propped open like everything was normal.

I whipped around and checked behind me before kneeling down to the ground. I checked the body for a pulse and found none. That's when I realized who it was. It was Max Spade. My main suspect, dead. "Double shit." I got up and felt around for a light switch on the wall. If someone was waiting in the shadows now would be the time to reveal themselves. I flicked on the lights and waited, every muscle in my body tense, my spine rigid. I stilled for a few tense breaths. No one was here. If they were, they had no interest in me.

I turned back to the body. Max was laying on his side, one arm and one leg splayed out. Judging by the rolling pin laying beside the body and the wound on the back of his head it was probably safe to say he'd been hit with it. There were more cooking supplies on the floor near the body

—a cutting board and another saucepan. Whoever had attacked him, Max had put up a good fight. He hadn't been taken by surprise, which meant either the killer wasn't terribly smart, or that Max knew him. Max had let him in before the struggle.

I leaned closer to examine the body again. Max's chef whites were stained and worn, but if I remembered correctly, they'd been like that before. His hat was gone revealing patchy gray hair. There was a long, deep scratch on his cheek. It seemed like someone had tried to cut him before giving up and grabbing the rolling pin. So they'd come in with a plan and had been forced to improvise. Either our killer was a poor planner—which was debatable based on what they'd done so far—or Max put up more of a fight than the killer had been expecting.

"Good for you, I hope you kicked his ass," I whispered. Another thing caught my eye. One of Max's hands was clutched in a fist while his other was more or less flat. Had he been ready to throw another punch, or was he holding something? I grabbed a towel to cover my hand and wedged his fingers open. It wasn't hard. Rigor mortis hadn't fully set in yet which meant that this murder must have *just* happened this morning.

Inside his palm was a diamond. I could tell immediately that it was real. I'd worked more than a few stolen jewelry cases and was forced to learn the difference the hard way. The jewel was large and set in a gold casing. I turned it over. There was a jagged imperfection in the center of the metal. Whatever had been attached to the back had snapped off when Max grabbed it.

Not many people could afford something like this, a real diamond. Not Max, not Miguel, not the staff.

"No way." Something was coming back to me. The other day when we were at the golf club interviewing Daryl Hackney he'd had on diamond cufflinks that looked *exactly* like this. Max must have grabbed at Daryl during the fight and pulled off one of his cufflinks in the struggle. "Well I'll be damned. Thanks, Max."

But how could it have been Hackney? He had an alibi for both the *theft* and the *murder*. Was I wrong? Had I made a critical error somewhere along the way?

It would mean either someone was lying for him or he was working with a partner. But who? If it was true that Daryl was working for Mr. Lazzo maybe he'd received some help covering up his crimes. Why kill Max, though?

I gazed down at the body. Poor, dumb, drunk Max.

He must have known something that would have pointed me straight to the killer. But why kill him *now*? And if he knew something, why not tell me on Saturday when we'd first interviewed him? Maybe he hadn't realized what he'd seen until later. So what was it? He caught someone skulking around in the hallway where they shouldn't be?

Hackney? Regardless, whatever he'd remembered had prompted our killer to silence him before I caught wind of it.

Or maybe Max was in on it too. *He* was the second suspect. Him and Hackney were in on it together and when Max started to get cold feet Hackney silenced him. That could work. We'd always thought it might have been two people. Max, working in the kitchen, would have seen anyone walking down the back hallways. He could have been handed the statue and gotten it out of the house while his partner went back to the party, providing them with a better alibi. Only Hackney hadn't been seen on the camera in the hallway during the time of the theft. How had he avoided it? Dean and I had only found one way in and out of the study. If there were actually *three* people working together I was going to have an aneurysm.

I replaced the diamond in Max's hand and took a step back from the crime scene. Either Max or Hackney could have been the one in the house Saturday morning who had knocked me over. They were both the right height and shape. Both could have ties with Mr. Lazzo, but my money was on Hackney. Like Dean had said earlier, he had all those hardware stores. It would have been easy to clean Mr. Lazzo's dirty money.

I called the police and this time Warner showed up in person. He didn't look happy to see me. "Why am I not surprised to find you at the scene of another murder?"

I frowned. "Uh, probably because it's my *job*?"

Warner leaned against the polished metal counter. "Well now that your client is out of jail I thought you'd be sucking up to him. I'd fire you too if you got me arrested."

"Out of jail?"

Warner surveyed the body. "Oh, did no one tell you? His friend bailed him out this morning. We're still going to build a solid case against him, but yes, he's a free man...for now." He glanced up to what must have been my surprised face. "Aw, he's offended. Did you have a falling out with your rich-boy psychopath?"

"He's not a psychopath," I snapped.

Warner held up his hands in defense, raising his eyebrows. "Wow, touchy. I know you need the money, Sun, but working for someone who would blow up their own car is a bit extreme."

I rolled my eyes at his stupidity. "You know he didn't do that."

"Well, you didn't exactly come to his defense, did you?" He cocked his head to the side. "So you must have *something* against him, if not the explosion that almost killed you, then what?"

I *almost* thought about telling Warner the truth, just to get him to shut up, only I realized that I wasn't pissed at Dean anymore. Lexi had been right. He'd lied to me and I was still mad about that, but Dean wasn't a *bad* guy. Just someone walking down the wrong path. He would never blow up a car to try and hurt me. And even if I put my own feelings aside, he would never hurt his precious Speedster either. The idea was laughable.

"Do you know where he went?" I asked.

Warner kneeled down by the body, inspecting Max's wounds. "I don't know. He said something about his uncle's house and cleaning up. The uncle we still haven't been able to contact, by the way. Not even the Greek police can find him. It's like he's fallen off the face of the planet."

"*Hmm*, how unfortunate. Are we done here?"

He looked up. "Whatever. We'll call you if we have any more questions. You didn't touch anything, did you?"

"Nope, nothing at all," I lied. I'd always been a good liar even though I hated doing it. Warner was the rare exception who I felt okay lying to. I *almost* threw him a bone about the diamond, but held back. Warner didn't need a leg up. I was about to solve this. Right after I confronted Dean.

EIGHTEEN

Dean was probably still mad at me for leaving him in jail. I almost felt bad about it. *Almost.* I drove the Jeep across Hollywood back into the hills. When I pulled up to the house I spotted Dean standing on the front porch looking down at his phone. There was no car in the driveway, and I was reminded that Dean's car was toast. He'd probably gotten an Uber here or Felicity had dropped him off. Did he really think that if he just finished cleaning up the house his *uncle* wasn't going to press criminal charges against him? For such a criminal mastermind he was in for a rude awakening.

I parked along the opposite curb behind a gray electrician's work van and jogged over to him. "Hey, Dean."

He whipped around, his face pinched with displeasure. "Oh, it's you." He narrowed his eyes. "You left me in jail."

"Yes, I did." There was a long drawn out pause, his gaze never wavering from my face. "Sorry about that." I shrugged. I hated lying, and I hated apologizing even more. I looked away first, turning my attention to the detailed shrubbery in front of the house.

His frown slowly melted, replaced by a small smile. "You're forgiven, I guess." He crossed his arms. "Are we even now?"

I shook my head. "No, not by a long shot, however I'm not pissed anymore. You'll never guess where I just came from." I filled him in on Miguel's alibi, Max's death, and about the diamond.

His jaw dropped. "Daryl killed Max?"

I shrugged. "That's the best explanation I can come up with. He must have faked his alibi somehow."

"*Hmm*, so what are you doing here, then? Shouldn't you be arresting Hackney?"

I rocked on my heels. "Yeah, only I kinda figured that if it was Hackney that was trying to kill us, then he'd probably be following you after you got out of jail."

He narrowed his eyes again, scrutinizing me. "Are you trying to tell me that you're using me as bait?"

I shrugged sheepishly. "Maybe?"

"And here I thought it was because you were *so* apologetic." He turned back toward the front door and then stopped, his hand on the handle. "This door was locked yesterday."

I walked up the porch steps to meet him. "Are you sure?"

He nodded. "I had a couple friends watching the place while I was in jail. This was *definitely* locked before."

I pulled out Tasha the taser. "I'll go in this way. You stay here."

He frowned. "Yeah, right."

I let out a deep breath. "Fine, you go around the back, but if you see Daryl running away, let him go, and then shout for me. Don't take any risks, Dean."

He grinned. "You know I wouldn't do that, Noah."

"*Right.*" We split up. Dean ran around the side of the house and I went through the front door. I pushed it in slowly, listening for movement. Did he know we were here? Had he heard the car pull up? Was he waiting in the dark to jump us? Also, what was he doing here at all? I'd been half-joking about using Dean for bait. Was Daryl setting some sort of trap to kill Dean? Tying up loose ends? Like with Max?

I took a few careful steps inside, crossing the blood-stained marble entrance hall. Nothing. No signs of a break-in other than the door. Had it really been locked before, or was Dean mistaken?

I walked down the hallway and turned into the lounge. All of the cleaning supplies were still sitting out from when Dean had attempted to clean a couple days ago. The room was otherwise untouched. Whoever was in this house had the upper hand. I clenched and unclenched my fingers while turning in a circle, surveying the rest of the space. It was dark without the blinds open and the lights turned off.

Clink.

A glass tumbler from the bar rolled off the counter and cracked onto the carpeted wooden floors. I jerked towards the noise and then a shot rang out.

Bang. Right near my ear. I dropped down on all fours and scuttled behind the nearest object—a plush velvet chair. *Bang. Bang.* Two more shots in the exact spot I'd been moments ago.

Shit. Focus, Noah. I had to get over to the shooter's side of the room. I crawled from one chair to the next, nearly losing my foot when another shot followed me. *Bang.* Wherever Dean was I hoped he was calling the cops and staying as *far away* as possible.

"Hey asshole!" Dean's voice carried across the room. He was standing in the second entrance to the lounge, closer to the shooter than me.

Oh, great.

"Yeah, *you*, Daryl Hackney. You might as well show yourself because you're not fooling anybody."

Out from the shadows came a laugh. The voice grew louder, "You idiots." The figure stepped out from the darkness next to the bar and into the light by the only half-drawn curtains. The figure was tall and square.

"Everly Sanderson?" Dean asked, his eyes wide.

She had a pistol pointed at his chest ten feet away. She was dressed in gray coveralls with a cap covering her hair. That's when I remembered the work van parked outside. She must have dressed like an electrician to sneak in through the front door since the security system was back up and working again. She pulled the hat off and smiled. "Daryl Hackney? You thought that rich asshole had the intelligence or skill required to steal one of the most valuable antiquities in Hollywood?"

Dean balked. "Oh, uh..."

"It wasn't a cufflink." I was finally putting two and two together and getting four. "Was it?" I said from my hiding spot. It was silly to hide now that Dean was in full view, so I stood up, tucking my taser away from sight.

That's when I finally noticed the bandage on her ear. Her face was bare, though she was just as beautiful, even with her lips twisted in a thin line. "Max pulled out your earring and you were dumb enough to leave it there?"

She looked like she wanted to wrap her hands around my throat and squeeze. "Turns out when you're high on adrenaline you don't notice certain things until it's too late." She laughed through her nose. "It doesn't matter. Those idiot cops aren't going to trace it to me."

Well, she was *probably* right about that.

Dean frowned, his eyebrows knitting together. "Who *are* you?"

She smiled and gestured with the gun for him to walk over to me. "The woman with the gun, *idiot*."

Dean stopped at my side and put his hand on the small of my back. "Are you okay?" he whispered.

"Peachy," I replied through gritted teeth. If he had stayed away like I'd asked I'd still have an advantage against her. Now she had a trained gun on us and she clearly wasn't afraid to fire it.

Everly took a few steps backward into the center of the lounge, right next to the coffee table where all the cleaning products were. "I have to hand it to you two. You certainly made this difficult for me."

Dean asked what we were both wondering. "Made *what* difficult?"

She edged over to the vacuum cleaner and started messing with it, the hand with the gun still trained squarely on us.

What the hell was she doing? Then it dawned on me.

She detached the old-school dust bag and reached inside, pulling out the gold cat statue worth almost as much as the house itself.

Dean's jaw dropped. "It was still here in the house the whole time?"

Everly frowned. "Yes, quite annoying. Everything was going perfectly the night of the party. My partner was waiting outside ready to take the statue from me, and then that bumbling drunk idiot, the chef, had to go and knock into me while I was making my way down the hallway. He was red as a tomato and on the verge of falling over. I couldn't risk being spotted by anyone else, so I searched for a place to stash the statue for a minute until I could return. The first closet I tried nearest to the kitchen was...occupied."

Dean giggled under his breath.

Not really the time, Dean.

"So I tried the next closet and finally got lucky. There were too many people walking around, that stupid social media kid and Conrad. I couldn't go back for it without getting caught again, so I decided I'd come back the next day."

"Until your partner turned on you," I filled in. "He knew you'd hidden the statue somewhere in the house and he came back early to look for it."

She smiled, though her eyes were narrowed. "That big oaf almost ruined everything. By the time I got here he'd completely ransacked the place. He *demanded* that I tell him where I'd hidden the statue and said that he'd kill me if I didn't." She laughed at the idea. "I told him my father wouldn't appreciate that."

"Your father?" Dean asked.

"Yes, Teddy Lazzo?" she said slowly as if we were too stupid to figure it out by ourselves.

"Oh, shit." Dean's eyes went wide. "You're Teddy Lazzo's daughter?"

She did a small curtsy. "Yes, and Herald, that big idiot, knew how important this was for me. To prove myself. My father has wanted this statue for decades."

It was all starting to make sense. "But you didn't have time to grab the statue that morning because we showed up."

She gritted her teeth, her jaw popping. "Yes."

"Then you couldn't get into the house because the police were all over it. And after that Dean had people watching the place until this morning when he got out of jail."

She grinned. "Thanks for moving the vacuum by the way. If I hadn't had to go looking for the damn thing I would have been gone already before you showed up."

"You left the front door unlocked." I shook my head. "Rookie mistake."

"Screw you," she spit out. "I'm the one with the gun," she glanced down at the golden cat, "and the statue. So from where I'm standing, there's only one amateur thief here and it's not me."

Dean scrunched up his face. "You knew who I was?"

She rolled her eyes. "Well I knew you weren't Mr. William's *nephew*. It didn't take long to figure you out, Dean Prescott. The cat burglar of San Francisco, the trickster of Pasadena, the charmer of West Hollywood.

Once I knew your *real* identity it wasn't hard to get myself invited to your little party."

He clenched his fist at his side. "Well, did you have to blow up my Speedster? That wasn't very nice."

She laughed. "That *was* fun. Even more so when the cops arrested you. I didn't think they'd *actually* do it, although that bunch don't need much help to make stupid decisions. Unfortunately my distraction didn't stop you two from creating even more messes for me."

"Yes, why *did* you kill Max? Did he start remembering things he shouldn't?"

She smiled, her eyes hollow. "He called me and told me he remembered seeing me with the statue. He might have been bluffing, but I couldn't chance that. Then he had the balls to *blackmail* me. He said he'd shut his trap for ten percent of the pot." She laughed again, her eyes rolling to the back of her head. "Ten percent of four million dollars?" She shook her head and pursed her lips. "I don't think so."

"Only, he put up a good fight?" I said.

She frowned. "Yes, I wasn't expecting that. He went feral on me as soon as he could tell I wasn't going to let him leave."

Dean's arm that rested on my lower back traveled down to my hand, to the taser. I gave him a subtle, yet stern, expression. He smiled, but didn't let go of his grip on it. "Yeah, trust is important in any partnership and it looks like you couldn't trust yours?" he asked.

Was he asking me to trust him? I was blocked by the chair in front of me, however he stood closer to her, if only by a foot or two. Dean found my gaze and winked.

Shit.

I let go of the taser and dashed off to the right, crashing right into the bar and breaking glasses everywhere. The distraction was good enough for a second or two. That's all Dean needed to run over to Everly and tackle her. They grappled over the gun and a shot went off into the ceiling, spraying plaster dust everywhere. I ducked down to the ground. She had to be short on bullets now. What was that, five?

I peered around the corner of the bar. Dean was on top of her, holding her arms. *Where's the taser?* Then she hit him in the head with the back of the gun and it stunned him long enough for her to regain the upper hand. She stood and trained the gun down on him. He stumbled to his side, one hand clutched against his temple.

"You have to take the safety off when you're trying to tase someone, *asshole!*" She grabbed the taser off the floor and slipped it into her back pocket. "Nice try." She gestured the gun at me. "You're going to stay right there or your friend is going to have an even worse *headache.*" She dragged Dean to a standing position and placed the gun up against his temple. She looked across the room. "I'm leaving, and you're not going to be following me. Got it?" She walked backward toward the door.

"You know I can't let you do that," I said, traveling a good ten steps behind her.

"And yet you will. You forget that I've been watching you for days." She grinned. "Dean Prescott is more than just your friend, isn't he?" She left the lounge and dragged Dean down the hallway.

Dean caught my eye. All his usual brightness was gone from his face. *Shit.*

" 'Course not. He's a client. A crooked one at that." I tried to put as much disinterest and power into my words as possible.

She wasn't buying it. "*Right.* Do you go around kissing *all* your clients?"

We turned the corner and entered the back hallway of the west wing. She must have been aiming for the side door by the kitchen—the same door she'd tried to use before to get the statue safely out of the house.

"Maybe I do, you got a problem with that?" If I could only keep her talking maybe she'd get distracted long enough for me to reach them. "You clearly have a lot of problems all on your own, you don't need any of mine."

Her lips twisted in a grim smile. "Shut up."

"I mean, stealing a four million dollar statue and killing two people just to try and make your daddy proud is a whole new level of daddy issues, isn't it? I guess he never hugged you as a child."

She furrowed her brow. "I said shut up, you annoying asshole. Whatever you're trying to do, it won't work."

Okay, so we'd watched the same detective shows growing up, got it. We were right in front of the study where the statue originally sat. Something was eating at the corner of my mind, only I couldn't remember what it was. *What is it?*

"You're not going to get away with this," I said, even though it was cliche. "Do you expect to kill us both and no one will notice?"

She shrugged. "They didn't care about the last two, what makes *you* so special?"

I jumped to the right and punched the button behind the picture frame. The metal panic door slammed down across the study doorway causing Everly to jump back a step. It was all I needed. I charged toward her, with Dean acting at the same moment. He slipped the taser from her pocket—remembering the safety this time—and tased her side as I snatched the gun from her hand.

She screamed into silence and dropped the statue. As the antiquity fell to the floor, Dean—in an act of Hollywood heroics— rolled onto the ground, reached out, and cradled the cat in his arms before it could hit the carpet.

I pulled Dean up, statue and all, and hugged him. "Are you all right? How's your head? Did she hurt you?" I examined him, searching for more injuries.

He cracked a grin. "I'm fine." He reached down and shocked her with the taser a second time. "That's for my car, bitch. Do you know how hard those are to come by? You destroyed a piece of history." She groaned, her eyes shut tight from the pain.

The drone of police sirens grew louder. I rolled my eyes. "Now they show up. Useless."

Dean beamed, clutching the precious statue in one arm and grasping my shoulder with the other. "Do we get to tie her up? Gag her?"

I frowned. "The cops will be here any second, Dean. I *think* we can avoid that."

He pushed out his lower lip and furrowed his brow. "Shame."

* * *

When the cops did finally arrive they were just as shocked that the thief and killer had been Everly. Everly *Lazzo*, as it turned out. Wanted in two states for bank fraud and grand larceny. Apparently she took after her father's side of the family.

When Warner showed up he was *not* pleased that we'd figured it out before him. Not that we'd done all that much figuring out. I was kicking myself that at every turn I'd been wrong. Always on the right track, and yet never close enough. If I hadn't come to the house to check on Dean what could have happened? I shuddered at the thought.

When Everly finally came to she tried to play the sweet and innocent card, only everyone knew her tricks by then. The crying and pleading didn't do anything to sway them. They clapped her in handcuffs and carted her off to the police station immediately. It was gratifying to see the police doing something right for a change.

"*Technically* we can't get her on robbery, only attempted robbery since the statue never *actually* left the house," Warner explained.

I hadn't thought of it that way, but I supposed he was correct. For once. All that preparation and all that scheming and the damn thing never actually went more than a hundred feet from the study.

"I'm assuming the two murders and two attempted murders will be enough to get her convicted?"

He smiled in a *you're a total dumbass and I hate you* sorta way. "Obviously. The state should have no trouble getting a conviction with your testimony of her confession. Or who knows? Given the right pressure, she might write the confession herself."

I crossed my arms. "*Hmm*, I don't know about that. She's Teddy Lazzo's daughter. If she hadn't been so confident she was going to get away with killing the two of us I don't think she would have said so much. I don't know."

He shrugged. "Give me twenty minutes with her. Then we'll see."

"*Okay.*" I laughed at his misplaced confidence and went to go find my annoyingly misguided, yet wholly well-meaning, client.

Dean was standing on the front porch, leaning against the railing. Even in a suit rumpled from a night in jail and a fight with a murderer he

270

still looked handsome, straight out of a GQ cover shoot. "Are you sure you're all right?" I asked him. The cops had more or less left now that the house had been swept through one more time. No more surprises.

"I'll be okay, maybe a bruise here or there. The EMT's said I might have a concussion."

I took a step closer and rubbed his temple with my thumb. "Yeah, she left her mark on you, didn't she?"

He smiled and reached out to touch my chest. "You too." My bruised ribs were singing with pain now that the adrenaline from the fight had worn off. "We're matching."

He laughed.

My smile faded into something I hoped appeared serious. "I'm sorry, Dean. I'm sorry I left you in jail even though I knew you didn't blow up your own car. I know you wouldn't do that. To me, or the car."

He grimaced. "Yeah, now I have to start the hunt all over again. Do you know how long it took me to find a Speedster in that kind of condition before?"

"I'm sure you'll figure it out."

He shrugged one shoulder and gazed down at his shoes. "Eventually, sure. I'm a little tight on cash right now, it would seem. My big payday with Mr. Hackney never happened because of all this mess. I'm back at square one."

I cocked my head to the side. "So what I'm hearing is that you're in need of a job?"

He smirked. "Why? Are you offering?"

I shrugged. "Maybe. Let's grab dinner, talk it over?"

He grinned. Even rumpled and bruised his smile did things to my insides. My chest tightened.

"Sure. That sounds nice."

NINETEEN

I patted down my shaved hair in front of the mirror and walked backward from the bathroom, only to walk straight back in when I realized I hadn't put on any deodorant. The bottle of cologne Dean bought me sat on top of the medicine cabinet. I thought about spritzing some on and then stopped myself. That would send the wrong message.

It was the next day, post arrest, post grueling hours long interviews about everything that had happened. Dean and I would both have to testify to put Everly in jail, and I was fine with that, even if Dean was a little skittish to be in court. He *technically* didn't have a record, and so there was nothing for him to truly worry about. He wasn't on the cops radar *at all* after it was confirmed that Everly had been the source of the *anonymous* tip.

However, there had still been the trouble of Mr. Williams who owned the house. He'd been set to come back from Greece in a few days and what a story he was coming back to. So I'd made a deal with Warner.

I pulled him aside yesterday and talked in a low tone. "This is a pretty high profile case."

He rolled his eyes as if I was a waste of his time. "Yes, *and*?"

"This should look pretty good for you...*if* you get the credit."

He narrowed his eyes. "What's your deal, Sun?"

"Simple. You downplay what happened to Dean's uncle when he gets back, and I'll make sure you get all the credit for solving this case— the arrest, the evidence, everything. I don't care."

He grinned. "What's to stop me from taking the credit anyway? This *is* my case."

I cocked my head to the side and stared him down. "I have a couple friends at the LA Times who owe me a favor, Warner. Come tomorrow, it can either be *my* name or *yours* splashed on the front page. It's up to you."

"Are you threatening me?" He *almost* looked impressed. "Goody two-shoes Noah Sun?"

I shrugged. "It's not a threat, it's just the facts. I know your department has been slow to close cases these past few months and you could use the boost."

He glared at me for several painful seconds. This was the only way I could keep Dean from being investigated further. The only way I could control the situation. I'd never played my hand against Warner before. I always let it go, let him win. Not today.

"Fine," he said through gritted teeth. "I get the credit with the commissioner and the press, and I'll do what I can to downplay what happened to Mr. Williams. *No promises.* It's going to be pretty hard to downplay murder."

I smiled. "Just tell him there was an attempted break-in and someone got hurt in the process, but that you arrested the culprits, and everything is okay. Simple."

"*Whatever.* Don't expect me to *ever* do this again. This is a one time offer, Sun."

"Got it."

Currently, I was late for dinner. Dean had insisted on picking the restaurant. I'd suggested Greta's diner, but he'd complained that it wasn't nice enough for a victory dinner. I supposed that's what it was—a victory dinner. We *were* victors. We'd solved the case. It only took two people dying, one car exploding, and many bruises on the both of us. Not to mention that after everything was said and done Dean had made a couple new enemies. Mr. Hackney was pissed that their business deal had been canceled, and now Dean had Warner on his tail. He'd be closer scrutinized if the cops ever suspected him of something again.

I'd made a new enemy of my own. When I'd checked the mail today I'd received a dark blue envelope. Something expensive. At first I'd thought it was from Dean or maybe Felicity, however, upon closer inspection, I realized the return address was blank. Inside was a small card of the same dark blue paper. In clear black script it said, "I see you." It was signed with the letter L. It didn't take a genius to put two and two together. Teddy Lazzo was pissed that we'd put his daughter in jail. I didn't want to contemplate what the repercussions of that would be, but I wasn't scared. Guys like him didn't scare me. They were all bark and no bite—mafia smoke and mirrors.

However, I did find myself checking my locks more often and making sure my cameras were in working order. No reason to take chances just because I wasn't afraid of the big bad wolf.

I arrived at the restaurant ten minutes late. The valet took my Jeep and I entered through the glass doors. This was a nice place. Much nicer than I'd had in mind. The ceiling was low and the room was dark except for the twinkling golden tea lights and glowing glass orbs over each table. The hostess took my leather jacket and directed me to our table. Dean was already sitting down, a cocky smile on his lips. "You're late."

"I know, I'm sorry. Traffic's a bitch."

"Not very responsible for my boss to be late to our first meeting."

I sat down and took a sip of the water in front of me. "Whoa, you're not officially hired yet, hotshot. I thought we were here to have dinner?"

He laced his fingers together on top of the table. "We are. And to talk about my future employment at the Golden Sun Detective Agency. It's not much of an agency if you only have one detective, huh?"

I smiled and sat back. "Okay then, Mr. Prescott. What do you feel like are your strongest skills that you would bring to the agency? Other than lying."

He blew out a fast breath. "*Oof*, harsh, Mr. Sun. I bring a lot to the picture. Not only am I a good *actor*, I know a lot of people. A lot of *rich* people. You need new clients and what you're bringing in currently isn't cutting it."

I raised an eyebrow. "How do you know that? I could be fabulously wealthy."

He laughed under his breath. "Okay, well, I've seen inside your apartment, Noah. Either you're a committed minimalist who hates cleaning, or you're a hard-on-your-luck professional who needs a nice payday. Which is it?"

I squirmed under his scrutiny. "The latter. What other skills do you have?" I asked quickly to change the subject.

He grinned, self-satisfied. "I thought so. What other skills do I have? Other than clients, I know a lot of other *professionals* that could prove useful during investigations like our last one."

I took another sip of water. The restaurant was warm and I was glad I hadn't kept my jacket. "You mean like Charlie?"

He nodded. "Exactly."

"And are any of these professionals criminals, Mr. Prescott?"

He placed his hand over his chest mockingly. "*What?* Of course not, Mr. Sun. They are all hardworking freelancers in need of employment, that's all."

"We'll put a pin in that for later. What else? Can you type?"

He nodded. "One hundred words a minute."

"Is your schedule flexible? Being an investigator means we keep odd hours. We could be working day or night."

He grinned wickedly. "Oh I'm pretty flexible, Mr. Sun."

I rolled my eyes. "That's something I wanted to bring up as well. What happened before...." I lowered my voice, "...with the kiss. Can't happen again. You would be my employee and we would have a strictly employer-employee relationship. Got it?"

He shrugged. "If you say so, boss."

I frowned. "I mean that, Dean. I already tried the whole partners who work together thing and it went disastrously. I don't need a repeat."

He gave me a small smile that told me he was holding something back. "Okay. Your agency, your rules."

The waiter came by and we ordered off the menu. I looked at the prices and set down the laminated sheet. "Dean, you didn't tell me how expensive this place was."

He laughed. "Oh lighten up, it's on me. This is a victory dinner; we're celebrating."

"Can we not celebrate with a burger and beers?" I grumbled.

"Of course not." He grinned. "What are we, animals?"

I got serious, schooling my features. "I need you to answer this next question honestly, Dean."

He read my expression and stopped laughing. He straightened in his chair. "Okay, shoot."

"If you work at the agency, you can't do anything that you were doing before. I'm offering you a chance to change your life, Dean. You work for me, you play by the rules. That goes for Felicity too. I won't get you guys in trouble if you promise to stay on the straight and narrow, earn some honest income."

He cringed. "About that..."

"*What?*" *What now?* What could he possibly tell me?

"Her name's not actually Felicity."

I rolled my shoulders, trying to relieve the tension. "Of course it's not. *Whatever.* My point is, from this moment forward you're no longer a con man. You're my assistant investigator. We'll start with a trial period. If you don't follow the rules or I catch you conning again, we're done. I believe in second chances, but no more. This is it, Dean."

He nodded, the smile gone from his lips. "I understand."

I let out a sigh. "Okay, good." I relaxed my arms that had been static resting on top of the table and grabbed my napkin to drape over my lap. "I don't want to know anything about what you did before. I'm technically obligated to turn you in if I have evidence that a crime has been committed."

"But you'd need evidence, right?"

I clenched my jaw. "Correct."

He grinned. "So say I, allegedly, stole your wallet in order to pay for this meal, what then?"

I automatically checked my back pocket and found it empty. "How did you—"

He laughed and tossed me the wallet across the table. "I'm only joking. I didn't take anything from you, I promise. I just wanted to see the look on your face."

I checked the wallet and everything was still there. "*Dean*."

"*Noah*," he said in the same stern tone.

I calmed myself and took another sip of my water. "Don't make me regret this, Dean."

"Oh I wouldn't dream of it." He grinned widely. "If you buy me dessert I'll even show you how I swiped it."

I cracked a smile. "Tempting offer; I think I'll hold off for now."

He shrugged. "You never know when it might come in handy."

"Oh I'm sure it will. I'm sure it will." I smiled and held up my water glass for him to toast. He clinked his against mine and we drank.

"To you," he said.

"To *us*," I amended. "And to your first case solved. May there be many more."

He beamed, and the light in his eyes made my stomach do that thing where it squiggled up into my chest and pinched my lungs, making me feel hot and itchy all over. This was either the best decision or the worst decision of my life. I guess I'd find out which tomorrow.

Author's Note

Thank you so much for reading How to Catch a Thief. I'm a self published author; I don't have the backing of a huge publishing company to help me out. So if you could please leave a star rating and a review, it would mean the world to me. Thanks a million xoxo, Austin Moon.

Acknowledgments

I love mystery. Plain and simple. And as long as I've loved mystery I've also wanted to write mystery. How to Catch a Thief is the first in what I hope will be a long series following Noah, Dean, Captain, Lexi, and Fern. I have so much fun writing these, so I hope you have just as much fun reading them.

I'm furiously working on the next book in my little hermit's den, so look out for that in the coming months! Let's just say it involves a cheating bastard, a murder or two, and lots of twists and turns I hope catch you by surprise.

What's harder than cycling hundreds of miles down the west coast? Doing it with the annoyingly hot guy who hates your guts.

Cal is excited to go on a two-week cycling trip with his best friends. He doesn't want, he *needs* the relaxation in order to kill his artist's block—he has a new show coming up and he's nowhere near finished.

However, things get complicated when one of his best friends brings her standoffish brother Nate along for the ride without telling him. Which would be fine if the guy wasn't a total pretentious jerk. Nate made sure to let Cal know that even though they are both gay they are *not* the same.

Sharing a tent with this guy every night is torture...until it isn't. Turns out getting the prick to smile does something to Cal he can't explain. Nate might just be exactly what Cal is looking for, whether he knows it yet or not.

Only 856 more miles to go. Can Cal and Nate make it to their destination without killing each other first?

Rough Waters

What happens when love gets in the way of business?

Berk is about to lose his job. In order to save himself and his expensive f-boy lifestyle he's forced by his overbearing boss to travel to the small, remote Ruby Island. The island is prime real estate for a new multi-story luxury resort.

Will has never left the island. He's been running the Ruby Inn with his aunt since his parents died, and business lately has been poor. When a new lodger comes to stay something sparks between them. That is, before Will realizes Berk is trying to destroy the only home he's ever known.

Can these two navigate the rough waters of love before the inn goes under?

About The Author

Austin Moon writes swoon-worthy queer romances and twisty mysteries. When they're not obsessing over their latest novel, they can be found crocheting, illustrating books, and cycling around their rainy little town in the PNW. Sip on a matcha latte and curl up with a good book during a thunderstorm for them, why don't you?

Amazon author page: Austin Moon
Goodreads: Austin moon
Instagram: @Austinmoonbooks
YouTube : @ryanwrites
Tiktok: @Austinmoonbooks